Metaphorosis

December 2019

Beautifully made speculative fiction

Also from Metaphorosis

Score – an SFF symphony

Reading 5X5: Readers' Edition
Reading 5X5: Writers' Edition

Best Vegan Science Fiction & Fantasy

Best Vegan SFF 2018
Best Vegan SFF 2017
Best Vegan SFF 2016

Metaphorosis Magazine

Metaphorosis: Best of 2018
Metaphorosis: Best of 2017
Metaphorosis: Best of 2016

Metaphorosis 2018: The Complete Stories
Metaphorosis 2017: The Complete Stories
Metaphorosis 2016: Nearly Complete Stories

Monthly issues

by B. Morris Allen

Susurrus
Allenthology: Volume I
Tocsin: and other stories
Start with Stones: collected stories
Metaphorosis: a collection of stories

Metaphorosis

December 2019

edited by
B. Morris Allen

ISSN: 2573-136X (online)
ISBN: 978-1-64076-153-7 (e-book)
ISBN: 978-1-64076-154-4 (paperback)

Metaphorosis
a magazine of speculative fiction
from
Metaphorosis Publishing

Neskowin

December 2019

The Martian in the Greenhouse.................7
by Geoffrey W. Cole

What Lies In Light...................................51
by Laura Duerr

The Dybbuk...107
by Lewis Gershom

Notes from the Laocoön Program...........145
by Phoenix Alexander

The Martian in the Greenhouse

Geoffrey W. Cole

"Can you sit?"

Honoré awoke to find herself lying on a cot in a little room full of mostly empty boxes of medicine and medical supplies. The woman who had asked the question loomed over Honoré. Pale, oily skin stretched tight over thick bones. Grey hair tied up in a bun. Ice-blue eyes set deep.

"Shush," the woman said. Honoré realized she'd been moaning in pain. It felt like she was steeping her extremities in hot tea. "The pain will go away. You'll keep most of your toes, and all your fingers. Our Doctor Madsen is very good."

Bandages wrapped Honoré's hands and feet. The woman offered her a small plastic cup full of awful-tasting water that she swallowed with difficulty.

"I'm the Captain," she said. "And you are Honoré." Honoré flinched as the Captain probed her arms. "You spoke in your sleep. We didn't know if you would make it. How did you find us?"

Honoré had another drink of the swamp-tasting water to buy herself time to think. She couldn't tell this stranger the truth: she didn't know where or even when she was. Revealing that she and her brother had tried to cheat their way to the future could only make things worse.

"You know about the pandemic?" Honoré said. A pained look across the woman's lean face told Honoré that she did. "It came for my mother first, then Benoît." Honoré's voice caught as she thought about that morning two weeks ago when they found their mother blue in her bed, soaked through with sweat. "I got sick not long after, but there was this company who offered to freeze anyone who was dying, for free. The last thing I remember is the bus ride to the old airport where they were doing the freezing. Then I woke up on the snow, all alone."

"How did you find us?"

"Benoît always said to look for a hill if I got lost," she said. "So I walked to the only hill I could find, and when I saw your station, I kept walking."

"So strong," the Captain said, her long fingers on Honoré's thighs. "Benoît is a beautiful name."

"Is he here?"

"On Mars?" The Captain shook her head. "Until last week, we thought there were only four of us on the planet. Now we are five." The Captain's cold fingers came to rest on Honoré's abdomen. "You are the one we've been waiting for."

Under the yellow light of grow lamps, the boy dodged between blackened beanstalks, pounced, and came up with a squirming mouse. He bit the animal's head off and Honoré thought she might throw up. Theo sucked, his chin running red, and when he was done, he offered her the still-warm carcass. She refused.

"Have you ever had pizza?" Theo asked as he peeled back the skin, cut out little slivers of flesh with his pocket knife, and lay them out in front of the electric heater.

"All the time," she said.

"What's it like?"

Honoré thought for a moment, then said: "Hot and chewy and salty."

Around a mouthful of mouse, Theo said, "That's how I'd describe mouse."

"It's not like mouse," she said.

He shrugged and went back to drying the meat.

Honoré worked the cold soil beneath the beanstalks. Her spade bounced off the concrete-hard earth, but this was her job now: till the soil, stir in the fertilizer, make the beans grow. *Look, Maman,* she thought. *I'm gardening on Mars.* It was all Honoré could do to hold onto her spade. Thinking about her mother made her ache. Honoré wanted to remember the woman Maman had been before the pandemic, but all she could picture was the delirious shell her mother had become in those last few days, mumbling about the old country as she drowned in her own fluids.

"That won't do," Theo said. He kicked at the soil where she was supposed to be working. "Here, like this." He took her spade and attacked the frozen soil until large clods loosened around the beanstalks. "Now dump the fertilizer."

Honoré wiped away her tears. She poured the bucket of viscous compost into the loosened soil, where the stinking liquid pooled about the withered stalk. The places where her big toes used to be ached. Her fingers in the gardening gloves were icicles.

"See?" he said. "Easy."

Theo plucked dead leaves and chatted while they worked: he told her about the latest videos and e-books the Captain made him study. Honoré barely heard him. Since awakening in the station a week ago, Honoré found herself constantly coming back to the fact that everyone on Earth was gone: Benoît, Régine, Marie N., Marie W., and Marie P. Everyone. Thirteen years had passed since the pandemic, the Captain said, and there had been no communication from Earth in that time. The only people on the planet were the four white people with whom she shared the shoddy station. She didn't know how to process this information. When she and Benoît had concocted their plan, they knew they would be leaving people behind, that the world would change when they were on ice, but with everyone getting sick, they thought they would see Maman again, and that at least one or two of their friends would join them in whatever future they awakened in. To be all alone, on a different planet, with everyone she knew gone, left her feeling like this was all some awful dream from which she would never awaken.

"That's enough," Theo said. The soil around her beanstalk was cut open. "Oswald will let you have it if you damage his roots."

Dinner was nothing like meals with Benoît and Maman. Those had been chaotic, hurried affairs, the food often burnt or undercooked, she and Benoît afraid to complain about the quality of the meal for fear of their mother either scolding them or bursting into tears.

In the month she'd spent on Mars, dinner was the same well-running operation every night, and tonight was no different. Honoré and Theo brought in beans and small brown lumps Theo insisted were potatoes, the Lieutenant carried in cubes of frozen grey meat from the freezer outside, the Doctor brought pinches of herbs from the uppermost level of the station, and they all placed their goods in the big pot of broth the Captain stirred. They ate in the control room, the penultimate level of the station that sat above the barracks where they slept, and below the observation deck to which Honoré had yet to be admitted. Windows along the far wall looked over the moon-lit landscape, frozen rock sprinkled here and there with white scars of snow. Honoré's ghost toes ached whenever she gazed out those windows for too long.

Honoré and Theo were given the largest portions, the Captain's slightly smaller, and Doctor Madsen and Lieutenant Oswald's portions smaller yet, just a few beans, a one-centimetre cube of meat, and a single brown lump each. Before they ate, they bowed their heads and recited together:

"We toil for the day
the red planet will be green,
We toil for the day
the water will flow,
We toil for the day we will
walk beneath the Martian sun,
We toil so that
our children may sow."

Honoré still expected them to say Amen, but they all just nodded their heads and dove in.

"Did you fix the CO2 scrubber, Lieutenant?" the Captain asked.

He hadn't; they were out of spare parts, but the exterior atmospheric oxygen levels seemed higher, as demonstrated by Honoré's survival, so he was enriching their atmosphere with small doses of Martian air.

"How many mice did you catch today, Theo?" the Captain asked.

Theo flushed red. He told her none, and instead spoke of what he learned in his tutorials.

"And how are our crops, Honoré?" the Captain asked.

As Honoré reported on her progress with the kale, she felt like she was answering a question from an overbearing teacher. All conversations in the station were like this: formal, unemotional, the adults using rank instead of name. Only Theo showed any signs of life. Honoré thought it might be a coping mechanism: these people had lost everything too, and had been dealing with that loss for longer than she had. Hiding behind formality helped her tamp down the yawning abyss of terror and grief that opened up whenever she thought too long about their situation; it must work for them too.

"Have you managed to get the meat-synthesizer working again, Doctor?" the Captain asked.

The Doctor winced at the question. Speaking seemed agony for him. The meat-growing equipment was still down, he said, so they would have to continue to feed off their frozen supply.

"And how about our new arrival?" the Captain asked the Doctor. "Is she ready?"

The Doctor went into a coughing a fit in response, a phlegmy, body-wracking affair that made Honoré lose her appetite. She looked out the window as the Doctor worked through his fit. Moonlight made the world beyond look dead. But that wasn't right. The glowing crescent sitting about the horizon looked just like the Earth's moon.

Honoré tried to remember what she'd learned a few months and thirteen years ago in her Cégep Explorations Science class. "I thought Mars didn't have a moon."

Everyone stopped eating. The Captain gestured at Theo, who recited: "It has two, Phobos and Deimos."

"That looks just like our moon."

"Low-orbit satellite," the Lieutenant said. "They launched it as part of the terraforming effort to help the seed organisms adapt to Martian conditions. Many of Earth's photosynthetic species are phototrophic: they climb toward the light, both night and day."

"With some things, we can adjust easily," the Captain said. "Take gravity — it is lighter here, and we barely even notice the difference. But the moon is hardwired into Earth's biology. Life can't survive without it."

Honoré accepted the answer. Every time she observed something strange about Mars, the Captain or the Lieutenant had similar answers. When she had spotted a star moving through the sky that looked just like a terrestrial satellite, the Lieutenant had explained that they had been launched from Earth and might contain more frozen people like her. One morning she spotted what appeared to be a passenger jet arcing across the sky, but the Captain explained that it was a robotic drone seeding the atmosphere with CO2 to start the greenhouse effect. And every time the Lieutenant or the Captain provided their perfectly rational answers, the breathless, irrational hope that took root inside her was stamped out.

After dinner, Honoré helped Theo clean. The Captain climbed the ladder that took her to the floor above the control room, and the Doctor followed. By the time Honoré and Theo were ready to dry the dishes, the Doctor returned, flushed, his hair damp. He poured himself a drink of water and hobbled to his bed. The Lieutenant came up from wherever he'd been working, cleaned his hands in the dishwater, and climbed the ladder.

The Captain and Lieutenant climbed down together as Honoré and Theo finished the last of the dishes. Cheeks glowing a healthy pink, the Captain shooed the men down to the barracks, then begged Honoré to join her at the kiosk where Theo did his reading.

"It's been over a month now," the Captain said. She clasped Honoré's hands as she spoke, as if the two of them were old friends. "Your arrival here has been just the thing we needed. You've injected an energy into our lives that has been sorely missing."

"Everyone has been welcoming," Honoré said.

"Theo, in particular, adores you. He talks about you every night."

"He is a fine boy," she said. The Captain smiled at that. Pride, Honoré thought. She'd always wondered, but now she was certain, even though she'd never heard the boy call the Captain 'mother'.

"Do you understand our mission, Honoré?"

"To build a home for humanity on Mars."

"And are we doing a good job of it?"

Honoré considered the sickly plants in the greenhouse, the failing solar panels, the defunct meat-synthesizers, Theo and his mice. But the Lieutenant was competent, the Doctor kind, the Captain assured. She didn't doubt them, but there was something else, whatever was hiding in their forced formality, that made her hesitate.

"I know," the Captain said. She patted Honoré's leg. "What we've built here is miraculous, but what is the point of a miracle if there is no one to share it with?" The Captain held Honoré's face between her cold palms so that Honoré couldn't look away from the woman's icy gaze. "I think it is time you helped us with our most important task."

The aluminium rungs of the ladder were frigid beneath Honoré's hands. The Captain was pretending not to watch as Honoré hesitated at the trap door that led to the uppermost deck. The Lieutenant worked on a piece of ventilation equipment. His hands were so dirty. Should she have chosen the Doctor first? The Captain said he was fading, that he had months, maybe weeks left. Tomorrow she would find out what it was like to sleep with a dying man. *No*, she thought. *I made the right decision.*

Honoré climbed into the observation deck. Artificial moonlight fell in through the windows that encircled the room. Drying herbs hung from the rafters, filling the space with the pungent odour of oregano and basil, scents that reminded her of Maman's herb garden.

"You don't have to if you don't want to," the Captain had said. "But you are so strong. Whatever they did to you while you were in cryostasis, they made you capable of thriving here. I always thought I would be the Eve of Mars, but after thirteen years of trying, we only have Theo to show for our efforts. Your babies will inherit the planet."

Honoré could see the entirety of human civilization from here: solar panels, greenhouses, the rover, and dry, frozen ground. It wasn't much of an inheritance. Her hands shook as she arranged the blankets and mattresses. They wanted her to get pregnant. To help restore humanity. The sex didn't scare her; she'd done it before, the first time a few weeks after her seventeenth birthday, because she'd wanted to know what all the fuss was about, and the second time was because she knew what all the fuss was about. What scared her was what getting pregnant meant. She realized that she'd been holding on to a vain hope that there was a real world she could go back to, but by sleeping with these two old white men, by letting them try to impregnate her, she could no longer pretend. This was all there was and all there would ever be.

She'd told Maman about sleeping with the two boys not long after the second. *Love is a gift*, Maman had said. *So be careful who you give it to. Not everyone is worthy.*

The knock on the trap door startled her. The Lieutenant's hands on the topmost rung were clean.

Wind shook the habitat. Honoré lay unsleeping in her bottom bunk. The Doctor wheezed in his sleep, Theo dreamed aloud about racoons and beefsteak tomatoes, the Lieutenant snored, and the Captain was soundless in her slumber. *They are your family now*, she tried to tell herself. *This is your home.* No matter how many times she repeated it, she didn't believe it.

Honoré readjusted the rolled blanket that elevated her hips. Had it been the Doctor or the Lieutenant tonight? She couldn't remember. Had it been two weeks or three since she'd first invited the Lieutenant up to the observation room? She couldn't be sure. Was either man worthy? *I don't know, Maman.* It would be her period again soon, though. The Captain said there was no point in trying during menses. Honoré had never wished for her period before.

The wind intensified and a massive tearing shook the habitat. Cold air that smelled of snow wafted into the barracks.

"Breach!" The Doctor yelled. "Breach!"

The others leaped from their beds. The Captain pushed Theo over to the ladder that led down to the airlocks and she wrenched Honoré out of bed.

"Get into the suits while we still can," she said.

Honoré slid down the ladder and ran over to the where the six space suits hung beside the airlocks. As she sealed herself away inside the bulbous helmet, where her own stench mixed with the stink of both the Doctor and Lieutenant and the odour of whoever had owned the space suit before her, all Honoré could think was how nice it had been to breathe fresh air.

Snow filled Bradbury greenhouse. Theo and the Captain hand-dug around the hydroponic equipment to salvage what they could, while the Lieutenant plowed a path around the greenhouse with the solar-charged rover. Honoré crawled over a massive drift and slid to the bottom, where she tried to dislodge a section of the greenhouse roof frame that had crumpled during the storm. The Doctor was trying to repair a chunk of loose siding in between coughing fits. *I will have to do my duty with the Doctor tonight.*

The thought filled Honoré with a sudden revulsion, and the revulsion turned to nausea. Puke was going to fill up the helmet, run all down her only pair of long underwear. She would stink for the rest of her life. Her gloves worked at the clasp at her neck. A hiss as the seal unclasped. She pulled the helmet off and vomited all of last night's grey meat and withered kale into the new snow. Then the nausea was gone. The cold air smelled like Christmas.

As she re-sealed the helmet, she realized what the nausea meant. She felt dizzy as she pulled the greenhouse roof out of the snow. She was pregnant. A baby was growing inside her, a baby that would call this place home, these people Papa and Grandmère. She began to cry without warning when she pictured her baby growing up here with only these strange men and women for family. No Benoît to bounce them on his knee, no Maman to feed them fried bananas. *Why am I so sad?* she thought. *This news will make everyone happy.*

She gave the plastic frame another tug and it slid out of the snow. A plastic envelope fluttered loose from the bent frame to land at her feet.

There was a packing slip within. Honoré unfolded the paper and read:

> *Ship to:*
> *Port Saunders*
> *Devon Island, NU, Canada*
> *X0A 3T9*
> *c/o Friends of Mars*
> *Martian Polar Simulation Habitat*

The date on the packing slip was seven months before the pandemic took Maman. She had to read it again, then again, until she started to understand, and once she understood, she had to force herself not to scream. She wasn't on Mars. All this time, they had been lying to her. The forced formality, the ritual before dinner, all of it was bullshit. Honoré had never felt so stupid. She'd known, all along, that something was wrong, yet she'd agreed to sleeping with those lying men. She'd let them get her pregnant.

"Sit-rep, Honoré?" the Captain said over the radio.

She had to stop herself from screaming obscenities at the woman. "Almost finished with the roof frame. Returning to the station soon."

As she trudged back through the snow, rage and betrayal making her blood run hot despite the Arctic cold, another emotion fought with the rest. Hope. Though she was stuck up here with these vile people, she was still on Earth.

She could go home.

Theo sucked up a snowflea that had wandered beneath the soy plants.

"Do you know how to drive the rover?" Honoré said. She was scraping the soil in the Bova greenhouse while he hunted.

"The Lieutenant promised to teach me on my thirteenth birthday."

"And when is that?" She let the cold soil sift between her fingers. The dirt fell no slower than it had when Maman made her help in the garden.

"Not for another six months." He stuffed another wriggling insect into his mouth and kept hunting.

Simulation, that's what the packing slip said. She vaguely remembered her science teacher talking about something like this. She'd thought people would have to be crazy to volunteer to spend a year inside a fake Mars habitat. The Captain, the Doctor, the Lieutenant, they were all a little crazy. During the chaos of the pandemic, they must have been forgotten up here. Abandoned. What better lie to tell themselves than the simulation had become reality? When a stranger showed up in the greenhouse, instead of face the truth, they'd built Honoré into their narrative: she too was part of a dying humanity's final effort to survive on Mars.

"Can you keep a secret, Theo?" she said.

"I've always wanted a secret to keep."

"I didn't get sick during the pandemic."

"So why were you frozen?"

"I faked it. It was my brother's idea." *Damn you, Benoît,* she thought. "After our mother died, he figured we could join her in the deep freeze and wake up all together in some brilliant future, so I forged fatal diagnoses for the two of us. This isn't exactly what we'd hoped for."

"Better here than Earth. Everyone down there is dead."

But they weren't dead. Those had been jets flying through the sky, satellites soaring overhead, the real moon glowing above the horizon. She could go home, and she would be damned if she let these people keep her here. The rover was solar powered. It could only travel a dozen or so kilometres on a charge, but that was further than a person could travel in this landscape. She couldn't ask the Lieutenant to teach her how to drive it, that might raise their suspicions.

"You know," she said. "My mother let me drive her car when I was twelve."

She spotted an earthworm wriggling in the soil and pulled it out. Theo's eyes lit up as she gave it to him.

"Twelve!" he said around a mouthful. "Rovers are way easier than cars. Wait until I tell the Lieutenant, he'll have to teach me."

Late one night a week after Honoré discovered she was pregnant, she crept out of bed and climbed up to the control room to use Theo's tablet. If she was going to find a way back to the real world, she had to be careful. She wouldn't be able to explain herself if the Captain caught her looking at maps of Devon Island, so she deleted her viewing history and only used the tablet when she had the control room to herself.

She'd already given up looking for any information on the Friends of Mars or their Martian Polar Simulation Habitat: all that information had been deleted from the off-line version of Wikipedia running on the tablet. Believing the lie would be a lot harder if there were constant reminders of the truth lying around. But there were maps of Devon Island in the off-line Google Earth, maps that filled her with a growing dread.

Devon Island had the distinction of being the largest uninhabited island on the planet. The island boasted a ghost town, a ghost mine, and a ghost science station, but no living settlements. From staring at Google Earth for so long, she'd put together the story of how she'd come to the island. Hundreds of thousands of people, both the dead and those diagnosed with terminal cases, had been frozen during the pandemic, and the company that did the freezing must have been looking for a cheap place to store them. The abandoned mine on Devon

Island would have done nicely. Somehow her coffin had been separated from the rest, had ended up out there on the snow, and after thirteen years, had gone into a revival cycle. She'd walked the rest of the way.

Walking back wasn't an option. When she turned the GPS function on in the tablet, it showed that they were located along the southwest rim of the Haughton Impact crater. The nearest settlement, an Inuit village called Resolute on Cornwallis Island, was two hundred and fifty kilometres away, and forty of those kilometres were frozen Arctic ocean. Theo had started his rover-driving lessons, but it would still be a long journey.

Honoré put down the tablet as nausea climbed her esophagus. She barely made it to the washbasin in time.

"Everything okay?" the Captain said. She was coming up the ladder from the barracks below, the blue light of the tablet reflected in her pale eyes.

"Bad potato."

"Could be," she said. The Captain poured a glass of water and handed it to Honoré. "Though it could be something else. You are late, aren't you?"

Honoré took a long drink and handed the empty glass back to the Captain.

"Late, yes, but not absent. My flow started this morning."

The Captain walked over to the kiosk where Honoré had been reading. The tablet shut itself off the second before the Captain picked it up.

"That's almost a week behind schedule," she said. "There can be spotting after conception. We'll get Doctor Madsen to look at you in the morning." She handed Honoré the tablet. "Don't stay up too late. Sleep is so important for a new mother."

Honoré wiped her index finger with alcohol-soaked gauze, and made sure to disinfect underneath the fingernail.

The Doctor knocked. "Ready?"

Honoré stuffed her shirt into her mouth, then pressed the sterilized finger inside her as far up as it would go and scraped. The pain was worse than she thought, but she didn't scream. Her finger came away crimson. She wiped off the blood with the gauze and tucked the gauze into her sock.

"Ready!" she said.

The Captain helped the Doctor into his chair, then helped Honoré into the makeshift stirrups.

"Be gentle," the Doctor said.

Honoré forced herself to relax as the Captain looked into her. "Is your flow always this heavy?"

"Since my first period."

"We'll keep trying, then," the Doctor said.

The Captain stared into her for a while longer, her gloved fingers so pale against the dark skin of Honoré's legs. "I think we need to redouble our efforts. Both men, each night when you are most fertile."

She peeled off the latex gloves and dropped them in the Doctor's lap.

Once the Captain was gone, Honoré put her clothes back on. The Doctor, as usual, kept his back turned.

"Do you know what's making you so sick?" Honoré asked, once she was dressed.

"Bacterial pneumonia. It's not my first bout, but we had antibiotics back then. I might fight this off on my own. If I don't, well, let's hope we can get a baby growing inside you before we get to that."

He tried to laugh but the sound came out as a crackling, convulsive shudder that turned into an extensive coughing fit. Honoré rubbed his back and tried to think. She couldn't do this alone, not if she wanted to bring Theo with her. She needed someone to show them the way. *Benoît, why did I listen to you?*

"There's something I want to show you in the greenhouse," she said. "Could you come with me?"

The Doctor leaned on her as they walked between the rows of wilting beanstalks. Honoré grabbed the small spade she used to break up the frozen ground.

"It's been too long since I've been down here," the Doctor said. "It smells like growing things. Like life."

She thought it smelled like shit.

They came to the place where the greenhouse walls had been patched.

"This is where we found you," he said.

"What if we could find antibiotics?"

"The nearest antibiotics are about 230 million kilometres away if my orbital calculations are correct."

"Resolute is two hundred and fifty kilometres away."

"What are you talking about?"

"The moon, the air, the jets, the gravity. Doctor, you know the truth. This isn't Mars."

The Doctor's eyes went wide and he began to cough.

"Real air will help." She slashed at the greenhouse wall. Cold wind blew in through the hole. He clamped a hand over his mouth, his eyes wild.

"Airlock," he said between his fingers.

He stumbled away from the torn opening, tripped over a kale plant, and fell.

"You can breathe," she said. "Stop pretending this is Mars! We're on Earth. You're safe." Honoré ripped his hands away from his mouth. "We can go home again."

The Doctor took long, ragged breaths of the cold air, each making his coughing worse until he was convulsing on his side, his face bruised, phlegm and blood on his purple lips. Panic reared up in Honoré as she tried to calm him down, but her efforts only made matters worse. She tried to drag him to the airlock, but the Earth's gravity and the Doctor's mass made the task impossible.

Halfway to the airlock, he let out a final, ragged breath, and went still. She couldn't find a pulse at his wrist.

Honoré ran to the airlock, cycled through, and screamed "Breach!" into the reeking habitat.

The Captain knelt on the floor of the locker room performing chest compressions on the Doctor's body, while the Lieutenant breathed through a plastic mask into the dead man's mouth. They wore their space suits without helmets. Theo and Honoré's space suits, and the Doctor's, and the other suit Honoré had never asked about, hung on the wall. Theo stood opposite Honoré, looking for all the world like he'd spotted a mouse in the corner of the greenhouse.

When the Captain fell away from the body, Honoré moved to take her spot.

"No," the Captain said. "There's no point."

The older woman leaned on her elbows as she caught her breath. The Lieutenant, sweat staining his brow as it did after their nightly duties, wiped his mouth with the back of his hands. Theo prodded the Doctor's belly with his index finger.

"He was very sick," the Captain said. She climbed to her feet and helped Honoré rise. "There's nothing you could have done. You had to think of the future of the species first."

"I didn't even think," Honoré said, the panic still there, threatening to overwhelm her, but she knew if she gave even the slightest indication that the Doctor's death was not what it seemed, she would never leave this place. "When he tripped and the spade cut through the wall, I didn't think. I just ran."

"The only thing I don't understand," the Captain said. "Is what he was doing in the greenhouse? A man in his condition shouldn't have been out in the cold."

"He wanted to see growing things," Honoré said. "He said he liked the smell."

"Who doesn't like the smell of human manure?" The Lieutenant barked out a laugh. "I should get to it. The work is easier before he gets too cold."

"The three of us will prepare the memorial feast," the Captain said.

Honoré risked one last look at the dead man from the ladder. She had done this.

Killed a man. It had been an accident, sure, but he had followed her out there because he trusted her.

The Lieutenant placed a hand saw beside the body.

Theo seemed excited as they washed potatoes. Honoré waited until the Captain excused herself to use the washroom before she asked why he was in such good spirits.

"The feast," Theo said. "It's the only good part about someone dying." Honoré's confusion must have been evident on her face. "Aren't you sick of frozen meat?"

Honoré forced down the panic as she washed the starchy lumps. Every dinner in the habitat, there had been those strange cubes of grey meat. From the broken meat-synthesizer, the Doctor had assured her, and she had taken him at his word. She had eaten human flesh daily, it was even now digesting in her gut, it was becoming part of the foetus they had tricked her into gestating. Panic turned to nausea. She might have betrayed the Doctor's trust by bringing him to the greenhouse, but he had betrayed her too, and his betrayal was monstrous. *No, Maman,* she thought. *He was not worthy.*

Her nausea intensified as she realized that she had to leave the habitat before the feast.

The Captain stirred the big pot while Theo set the table. Honoré hated that the stew smelled so good. The Lieutenant was still down in the locker room, humming oldies as he worked, but the sound of sawing had been replaced by hissing as the airlock opened and closed several times.

Honoré placed her hand on the Captain's stirring arm. "Can we talk in private?"

"Run down to the barracks, Theo," the Captain said, without looking at her son. "Find a passage in the Doctor's copy of Martian Time Slip that will be suitable for a reading."

Theo slid down the ladder.

"With the Doctor gone," Honoré said. "I'm worried that I will never get pregnant."

"We will have to get the Lieutenant to redouble his efforts." She took a sip of the stew, made a face. "Too bland." She added more salt.

Honoré tried not to clutch at her stomach. "What if the Lieutenant is the problem? I need to do what you never could."

The Captain stopped stirring. "He is just a boy."

"He will be thirteen soon. Old enough."

The Captain lifted the spoon, tasted, and offered it to Honoré. "Too much salt?"

A chunk of Doctor Madsen floated in the oily broth. Honoré let the liquid touch her lips and suppressed a gag.

"It's fine," she said.

The Captain stirred the meat back into the stew. "In the primordial days on Earth, the mother-in-law would often perform midwife duties. We are in the primordial days here, aren't we?"

Wind whipped the habitat and hissed through the patched holes.

"I think we should start today. Before the meal." The Captain looked ready to protest, but Honoré couldn't contain herself much longer. When they served the stew, she wouldn't be able to keep pretending. She had to get out, now, while she still could. "What better way to celebrate the loss of one life than to conceive another?"

The Captain lifted the spoon and slurped down the steaming contents.

"You're right," she said. "It's fine."

The oldies the Lieutenant was humming cut out when Honoré stepped into the locker room.

"You're not supposed to be down here," he said. He was scrubbing a dark stain on the floor with wadded rags.

"The Captain wants you to talk to Theo," she said. "The two of us, Theo and I that is, we're going to do our duty before dinner. I can clean up here."

The Lieutenant showed no surprise. Humming "Doo Wah Diddy Diddy", he handed Honoré the wadded rags, washed his hands in the mop water, and climbed the ladder. As he did, she understood that his stoicism, which she'd always taken for strength, was something else. The man had never shown any emotion in the time they'd spent together, not even in their lovemaking. He had just cut his friend into bite-sized pieces, and he was humming a song as if he had been soldering a broken solar panel.

Honoré's hands shook as she scrubbed. If the Lieutenant was a sociopath, what did that make the Captain? Honoré wouldn't wait to find out. Once she was certain the Lieutenant had climbed the two floors to the control room, she opened his toolbox and took out a hammer and screwdriver. She placed the Captain's helmet on the deck, covered the bulbous faceplate with the rags, and tapped the screwdriver's head through the glass. The rags muted the crack. Her hands were shaking so badly that she dropped the screwdriver when she tried to break the Lieutenant's faceplate. The noise sounded like a gunshot and left her gasping for breath, certain that she would be discovered, but there was no movement upstairs. She forced herself to slow down as she finished the Lieutenant's helmet, the Doctor's, and the other helmet no one wore. Then she put her spacesuit and Theo's into the airlock with the tablet, and opened the outer door.

When she climbed up into the control room, everyone was looking at her. Had they heard? None of them said anything.

"Ready, Theo?" she said.

The boy nodded.

Honoré walked over to the ladder that led up to the observation deck.

"Give me a few minutes to get myself ready," she said. "I'll knock when I am set."

Honoré tied together the last of the blankets that had carpeted the observation deck, and lashed one end to the wall struts. There was a moon tonight, full and bright. *Low-orbit satellite, my ass,* Honoré thought. At least it would light their way. She loosened the screws holding the window above the place she'd anchored the blanket rope. The rover sat below, as charged as it would get after the brief stretch of daylight.

She knocked on the hatch and helped Theo through. Before she closed the hatch, she saw the Captain staring up at her. She mouthed "Don't worry" to the Captain and locked the hatch behind her.

Theo's hands trembled, his breath shallow. He walked over to the window. "I always wondered what it looked like up here."

Honoré joined him at the window and took his hand. "Do you trust me, Theo?" He nodded, his eyes wide. Just a boy. What mother would let her child do this? "They've been lying to you since the day you were born. This is Earth."

Theo tugged his hand away. "Don't joke around."

"The drone seeders, the fake moon, the satellites. All lies." She handed him the packing slip. "I found this after the storm."

He looked skeptical as he read, his eyes moving over the words again and again. "This is a trick."

"I'm leaving, Theo. And I want you to come with me."

He moved toward the hatch. "I can't survive out there."

"Yes, you can."

"I won't go."

He dropped to his knees beside the hatch and reached for the lock.

"Pizza," she said. "As much as you could ever want."

Theo settled back on his knees. "They tried to radio Earth. No one answered."

"It was a terrible time, but there are still people out there. They just forgot about you." She took his hand again and led him back to the window. "Do you trust me?" she asked again.

She hesitated at the window, thinking of the Doctor's gasping demise, but Theo was stronger than the Doctor. She threw open the window. Theo instinctively reached up to cover his mouth, but Honoré wouldn't let him.

"The air is wonderful," she said. He took a deep breath, coughed, then took another. "See?"

"What's going on up there?" the Captain shouted from below.

"We have to take her with us," he said.

"We can come back for her, once we are safe. But you know she will never let us leave if we don't go now. Will you come with me?"

The Captain screamed and pounded on the other side of the airlock door as Honoré gathered up their space suits. Honoré hobbled across the frozen ground, her socks sticking to the snow, and met up with Theo as he descended the last few metres on the blanket rope.

"We can put the suits on once we are far enough away," she said, trembling from the cold and adrenaline. "But we have to get the rover going now."

Theo climbed into the driver's seat, Honoré in the passenger's. The space suits filled the small compartment behind them. Theo's hands shook on the steering wheel as he tried to get the rover moving.

"Come on," she said.

"The Lieutenant only let me drive twice."

The airlock door opened and the Captain ran out in her space suit. She held one hand over the hole Honoré had punched in her faceplate.

The rover hummed to life.

"Move," Honoré shouted.

Theo was looking in the rearview mirror as his mother approached. Honoré reached across Theo and locked his door, then locked her own.

"Don't you take him," the Captain's voice crackled over the rover's radio. "Don't you take our future."

"Go, Theo!" Honoré said.

The Captain pulled on the driver's door handle. Theo stared, eyes wide, at the hole punched in the Captain's faceplate.

"You can breathe too," he said.

"The seed organisms," the Captain said. "They're building atmosphere."

"More lies," Honoré said. The Lieutenant stepped out of the airlock with a strip of duct tape over the hole in his faceplate. "This is Earth, Captain. You know it."

The Captain clawed at the door. "We took you in, Honoré. We made you part of us."

Honoré stamped on what she hoped was the gas pedal. The rover jolted forward, knocking the Captain to the ground. Theo pushed Honoré away from the rover's controls.

The Captain rose to her feet and ran toward the rover. "Don't leave, Theo. We are building a better world. All of it will be yours."

Theo froze behind the steering wheel.

"Please," Honoré said. "I don't want to have my baby here."

"You're having a baby?"

Honoré nodded. "I want her to see everything you learned about in your tablet. The cities, the mountains, the ocean. I want you to see it too."

Theo wiped away tears and hit the accelerator. The Captain screamed behind them.

"I want to eat a meat lover's pizza," he said. "And a Hawaiian."

The Captain was pleading with Theo to come back, when Honoré found the controls for the radio and flipped it off. The rover squeaked and rattled as it rolled over the frozen Earth.

Sea ice stretched to the horizon ahead of them. Theo stood in his too-large space suit beside Honoré, the two of them gazing at that great expanse of frozen Arctic Ocean. Behind them, the rover's solar panels converted the last long rays of the setting sun into the metres they would cross that night.

"How far is it?"

"Three days," Honoré said.

That was being generous. The days were getting shorter, only giving them enough charge for a dozen or so kilometres. The tablet told them that Cornwallis Island lay 40 kilometres across the ice, but using the tablet to navigate hadn't been foolproof to date. There was a good chance they would be spending several extra days out on the ice.

"What do we do when we reach the other side?"

"We follow the coast South until we get to Resolute."

Where, she told herself, there would be people. Real, living people. There had to be.

"Think they'll have pizza there?"

"Sure," she said. "But it will probably be frozen."

They climbed back into the rover, stowed their helmets, and drove out onto the sea of ice.

See Geoffrey W. Cole's story "The Martian in the Greenhouse" online at Metaphorosis.
If you liked it, leave a comment. Authors love that!
Remember to subscribe to our e-mail updates so you'll know when new stories are posted.

About the story

"The Martian in the Greenhouse" was originally a chapter from my novel, *Perpetua*. In the novel, the main characters are cryonically preserved in a mine similar to the one Honoré was sent to in "The Martian in the Greenhouse". The scene ended up being cut from the novel, and I thought the story was much more compelling with a young female protagonist than a middle-aged male, so I turned it into a stand-alone short story. I'm delighted to have it appear in *Metaphorosis*.

A question for the author

Q: What kind of non-fiction do you like to read and how does it affect the fiction you write?

A: Most of the non-fiction I read is either in audio-book or podcast form. Hardcore History, Radiolab and Science of the People are some of my favourite podcasts. I also like to read non-fiction books on astrophysics, indigenous issues, advances in biology and medicine, etc. The non-fiction material typically doesn't have a direct impact on what I write; the effects are more organic. One evening while walking the dog, some factual story I read ages ago will mate with a fictional idea that has been percolating in the back of my grey matter. If the offspring of the fact and fiction is relevant to the project I'm working on, I'll incorporate it; otherwise, it goes into the big 'To Write' file that is growing faster than I will ever be able to complete it.

About the author

Geoffrey W. Cole is an award-winning author, an engineer, a father of three, and a loving husband. Previously, he was a Segway tour leader in Rome, a Lego robotics instructor, a grizzly-bear handler, and a rock-n-roll singer. He enjoys back-country skiing, surfing, canoeing, cycling, roleplaying games, board games, fencing, running, and staring at trees. Geoff has degrees in biology, engineering, and an MFA in creative writing. He lives in Toronto, Canada. Geoff is a member of SF Canada and SFWA. Visit Geoff at www.geoffreywcole.com.

@geoffreywcole

What Lies In Light

Laura Duerr

I dream about the volcano again. The broad bowl of its crater is filled with shimmering light. I am standing at the rim like always, watching the warm and welcoming glow eddy and dance just a few feet below me in a swirling ocean of opal. I keep thinking I can see something beyond, or under, or within the lights, but it's too distant to view clearly.

I hear voices, too. That's new. The voice sounds like my brother, David, back on Earth.

He's weeping.

I kneel and stretch out my hand toward the light. Maybe David will reach up and grab my hand and I can pull him out. Even if he's not there, I'll finally touch the lights, after dreaming of them for so many nights. What will they feel like? Will they cling like mist to my skin, or wisp between my fingers like a breeze?

I never find out. I wake with my brother's sobs ringing in my ears.

It's sunrise on our fifteenth day on Janus. Through my small window, I can see the roof of the rover garage and a butter-yellow sky. The utilitarian gray blocks StellBio used to construct their research facility look misplaced among the fuchsia palm trees and coral-pink grasses that flourish on this island.

I sit down in front of the computer, which displays the StellBio logo as it wakes up: the stars of the Big Dipper multiplying and twisting into a DNA helix. Once the computer finishes reminding me whom I'm investigating, I open my messages. There's still only one: the message I received from David on our fourth day here.

David and my mom each had their reasons for not wanting me to take this job. My brother is tired of not knowing where in the world I am; my mother likes to be able to get drunk and call me to complain about why I'm not dating Logan anymore and why she doesn't have grandchildren yet.

Before I was called to take part in this investigation, I was working in a cubicle maze in Berlin; before that, a cubicle maze in Kyoto. I stopped dating Logan three years ago, after I realized I was happier in relationships with women. Mom kept needling me to quit working and settle down with a nice man and neither Berlin nor Kyoto were far enough away from her and her expectations. I keep hoping Janus is.

At least she hasn't called me, though I'd rather have endured daily calls from her than what I got from David.

I take a deep breath and open his message. My brother's face is pale and distorted by flickering waves of static. It's the same pattern afflicting the StellBio footage I've spent the last two weeks studying. The audio, at least, is unaffected, though by now it's burned into my memory:

"Hey, Rosa. Um... Dad died." David rubs his face and stares off to the right of the camera. "He, uh... He'd written you out of his will. Looks like he did it a long time ago, when he, uh, found out about you. Look, I didn't want you to find out like this, but Mom said you should know right away—"

I shut the message off; the sting is still fresh. I wasn't surprised Dad did what he did, nor was I surprised that Mom would want to inflict the knowledge on me as payback for the way I left things. What does surprise me is how much I still care.

As I get dressed, I hear the door across the hall open and close. It's probably Colin, heading to the biology lab to tend to his patient: the infant thunderer we rescued from a nesting site that had been attacked by Janus' primary predators. It was wounded, and from what we can tell, what remained of the herd left it behind.

StellBio gave the herbivores a more official name than "thunderer", but it's long and absurdly Latin, so we gave them our own name. They behave like cows and are vaguely cow-shaped, but that's as far as the resemblance goes. Maybe scaled-down cows with dinosaur tails, participating in a drag show.

What interested StellBio wasn't the herbivores themselves, but the feathery gold tufts of fungus that grow on their backs. The StellBio scientists on Janus claimed aliens like the baby we rescued could host the basis for anything from anti-aging cosmetics to a cure for cancer.

Then everyone on Janus disappeared, as did more than half of the thunderers on the island. StellBio claimed—or feigned—ignorance, hence the multinational investigation into StellBio's activities on Janus. Whatever miracle cure StellBio might have discovered, they won't be the company to bring it to fruition.

It's a clear day. I breathe in the warm, cinnamon-scented island breeze as I walk to the cafeteria for breakfast. We are now halfway through our scheduled mission. The ship that brought us here, now parked like just another building behind the rover garage, is programmed to power up and bring us home in fifteen days, and not an hour sooner. Beyond the ship, the black cone of the island's volcano rises innocently against the brightening sky.

Someone nudges me: Colin, the investigators' top pick for a large-animal veterinarian—an essential role, given how key the thunderers were to StellBio's research—and the youngest person on our team. He acts like it, too, waking up each morning cheery, still as ruddy-cheeked as the day he left the pastures of Queensland. Even worn out from emergency surgery on an infant alien, he's chipper.

"Morning, Rosa!"

"Hey, Colin."

He cocks an conspiratorial eyebrow at the volcano. "You've got cameras on that thing, right? In case it blows?"

"Lot of good it'd do, since our ship won't let us leave early."

"Couldn't cameras at least tell us which way the lava's flowing?"

I hesitate. "You'll think I'm crazy, but I'm not sure there's lava in there."

He grins. "Weird alien lava, then?"

"For starters, StellBio took down those cameras—"

"Of course they did."

"But I found surveillance footage showing the crater, in a folder someone at StellBio marked for deletion."

"What did it show?"

"The crater looked…white." It's hard to describe what I saw, particularly because the footage, like all the other video I've been working on, was in bad shape. "Like it was full of white light, flashing different colors."

"You're right," Colin says with mock seriousness, "I do think you're crazy."

"I'd show you, but the lights did something damaging to the camera. It's like staring into a strobe light."

He raises one eyebrow. "You said StellBio had deleted this stuff?"

"Tried to. I managed to find it."

"Cheers, then, Nancy Drew—you found the one thing StellBio deleted just 'cause it was bulldust and not because they were covering something up!"

I think they are covering something up —and not just the disappearance of their staff—but I stay quiet. He's probably right that the footage had been deleted simply because of its quality, not its content, but I suspect the latter. The damaged footage showed the lake of light I've been dreaming about ever since we arrived. I've never seen the volcano's caldera in person, but somehow it's gotten into my mind, and I think StellBio might have known why.

"How's the baby?" I ask, hoping to change the subject away from my conspiracy theories.

"Recovering   beautifully,"   Colin responds, "but she might be an orphan."

"How do you figure?"

"I couldn't bring any of the tracker tags online, so I looked through that footage you sent over, everything from when StellBio was keeping the thunderers in pastures up to the newest footage from just yesterday."

StellBio quickly discovered that the fungus they were so interested in only existed in a symbiotic relationship with the thunderers, and only in the wild. They couldn't grow the fungus in the lab, and apparently when they tried to domesticate the thunderers, the fungus never appeared, and the animals grew up weak and sickly. StellBio then began tagging the thunderers and returning them to the wild. As far as we can tell, they never got a chance to see if the released animals grew the fungus— people began disappearing just a couple weeks later.

"What did you find out?" I ask.

"Well, you weren't kidding about how badly corrupted that footage is."

"That's what I deal with every day here. Sure you don't want to trade jobs?"

"We're pretty sure Ripley's herd is gone. The reapers just annihilated them."

The predators also have an absurdly Latin name. We call them 'reapers'. It describes them pretty thoroughly. Despite the grim news, I have to smile. "Ripley? As in, 'believe it or not' aliens?"

"As in Ellen." He grins. "'Alien'. Figured we should name our baby after a survivor, right?"

"Makes sense. So where is Ripley going to go next? Will another herd take her in?"

He shrugs. "Hard to say. And the proximity of the attack is concerning. We've never observed the reapers so close to the facility. There're thunderers all over this island; I can't figure out why they went out of their way to attack the ones here."

"Sounds like a question for Saida."

"She's out searching for their trail right now." He looks closely at me. "You all right? You look tired."

I laugh. "Sorry, I forgot to pack concealer for my interstellar video analyst job."

He chuckles, hands raised disarmingly. "Not trying to start anything—we're just a few light-years from any decent counselors, so I wanted to check in."

"I'm fine." The lie rolls off my tongue as easily as ever.

"Well, if you need a break from staring at screens, you should come meet Ripley. I think she's ready for visitors, and she's damn cute."

"I'll think about it." I move to enter the cafeteria, but Colin is lingering.

"Rosa, you sure you're alright?" he asks.

What's the worst that could happen if I tell him? Sometimes people have bad dreams and they sleep poorly. It's not such a big concern. Right?

"I keep having weird dreams," I admit. "About a lake of light. I dream about it almost every night."

Colin glances around. "I do, too. I thought I was going crazy."

"And the fact that we both dream about it makes you feel less crazy?"

He grins. "Well, at least I won't be the only one. Any family history I should know about?"

He's teasing, but he comes so close to the truth that I can't laugh. His smile fades.

"Sorry. I wasn't, uh…sorry."

"It's okay. Family's just not…"

"You've never really spoken about them."

I imitate a breezy shrug. "Well, they were enough for me to take a job in a different solar system, if that tells you anything."

"Sorry to hear that."

I nod. I want to get out of this conversation and back to work—back to evidence of the volcano. If Colin is dreaming about the crater, then Huy and Saida might be, too. Maybe the StellBio employees were as well. "If you need me, I'll be in my lab."

"You don't want to see Ripley?"

"Maybe later."

After breakfast, I make one more stop: the pharmaceutical lab. StellBio originally loaded their facility with all manner of scientific instrumentation and experts in everything from linguistics and sociology to epidemiology and ecology to physics and geology. Back then they were Stellar Enterprises, sending ships through the wormhole they discovered, prepared to study—and hopefully profit from—whatever they found on the other side. After they discovered the fungus, the facility's resources were entirely devoted to its study. Now only two of the labs are in use: one for investigating the thunderers—Colin's specialty—and one where Doctor Huy Thahn tries to decipher StellBio's research on the fungus.

Huy waves at me when I stick my head in, but he's in conversation with the fourth member of our team: Saida, on the other end of a very garbled video call from one of the rovers. Her face fills Huy's display like a beautiful Picasso, the choppy transmission breaking her down into sparkling brown eyes and omnipresent black headscarf. She's a predation specialist, a household name to nature documentary fans, and she splits her time between research in the field and consulting on big-budget documentaries with celebrity narrators.

When I first saw her on the ship that brought us from Earth, I thought it was an amazing coincidence, but it turned out that the real reason the investigators called me was Saida. She remembered working with me on a gig for the BBC nearly seven years ago, back when I thought I wanted to be a documentarian. Someone on that crew took issue with Saida in a way that could have been dealt with by HR if we were in civilization, but we were in the middle of the Amazon, so I dealt with it with my fist.

Apparently that made a good enough impression on Saida that when she heard the investigation needed a video editor, she gave them my name.

I still need to thank her. That she remembered me at all is flattering; that she recommended me for a job like this is humbling. Did she notice—or does she remember—that I fell hard for her?

"Say again?" Huy is saying, frowning. "All four of the tagged thunderers in that herd were killed?"

"Yes—trackers are dead," she says. "And I've gone practica—all the way to the volcano—no sign of any other thunderers."

"Colin wasn't able to bring their trackers online," I say, loud enough that Saida can hear me. "I guess now we know why."

"Oh, hey, Rosa—seen the baby yet?"

I smile back. "I hear she's cute." I see Saida's jumbled features morph into a smile.

Huy spins his pen between his fingers. "The rest of the herd must've gone somewhere. The reapers wouldn't slaughter an entire herd like that—would they?"

Saida shakes her head. "Abnormal pred—behavior wouldn't be—weirdest thing we've—een on—"

"Saida, you'd better come back," I call. "We're losing your signal."

"It's that damn volcano," Huy says with unexpected vehemence. "The closer we get to it, the worse our signals are."

"Don't worry—urning back soon." The screen goes dark. Huy is already back to work, swapping petri dishes in and out of a microscope. He looks like he's not in much mood to converse. Then again, if I were the microbiologist responsible for delivering on a promise to find a cure for aging, I would be stressed, too.

I've set up my video lab in the facility's security office. All their data, including the archived footage from two dozen security cameras across the island, is backed up here. I've been trying to recover what seems to add up to several terabytes' worth of missing footage, while simultaneously attempting to clean up the quality of the footage that remains. About half of it has been damaged or degraded, and it's finicky about my scrubbing and deconvolution algorithms.

Plus, it isn't just the archived footage, it's ongoing. My message from David was affected, and the bank of security monitors ripples with a flickering distortion. Today it's stronger than it usually is, a pulsing flutter like a sporadic tremor.

There are many possibilities for what could be causing the distortion, like competing signals, solar flares, or electromagnetic variations. Those are just the possibilities I can make an educated guess on—and I feel like StellBio wasn't the type of company to be unprepared for any of them.

Which brings me back to my earlier suspicions: that StellBio knows more about what happened here than they admit. Maybe the missing footage was deliberately destroyed. Maybe something, or someone, else is on Janus with us, and their signals are interfering with ours.

My bracelet pings me. Originally it was only designed to communicate with the four drones I brought with me for additional surveillance, but I programmed it to operate on StellBio's frequency. I tap it and Saida's face appears, the projected image suspended over my wrist. I can barely tell it's her beneath all the distortion.

"Saida? Where are you?"

"—just found two more dead—erers. These—kill—several weeks ago—you still hear me?—important."

Two more dead thunderers, from a different herd? It doesn't sound that important. "Maybe it should wait until you get back."

"Rosa—both tagged." Her image jostles —she's driving fast, trying to get back into range. "There's no sign—other dead animals. It almost—they were targeted."

"Saida, just come talk to me when you get back, okay? The signal is too choppy."

"Keep—eye out for reapers," she said slowly, so most of the message gets through. "If they're somehow target—our signal—the facility itself could—danger."

She hangs up. I can't remember whose idea it was to start referring to the predators as "reapers," but it makes me shiver every time. The creatures are bipedal, reminiscent of ostriches but with arms that end in scythe-like claws—hence the reference to the Grim Reaper—and tongues that lash out with paralytic saliva. They are swift and talented killers, certainly capable of slaughtering an entire herd of their prey. The only question would be why—and Saida's theory is alarmingly plausible. After all, there are creatures on Earth that navigate using senses humans don't possess. Maybe the reapers can detect the radio tag signals.

But why would that drive them to mass slaughter?

I raise my bracelet again and key up one of my drones. I've been storing them outside the rover garage for quick deployment, and I watch as the big building falls away beneath the rising drone.

I send a series of coordinates: the nest where we found the injured infant, the four known reaper dens in this quadrant of the island, and the approximate location where Saida called about the other dead thunderers. Maybe the drone can find what StellBio's stationary cameras can't, and tell us where the reapers have gone—and when they might be coming back.

Then I return my attention to StellBio's bottomless archives. Our research can't keep turning up more questions. Somewhere among all the bytes and pixels they tried to erase are the answers we're seeking.

"Rosa!"

I jolt awake. I've dozed off in front of my wall of monitors.

Saida hasn't noticed. "You have to see Ripley eat," she says, laughing. "It's the cutest thing."

From the clinic next door, I can hear Ripley keening. It sounds like a cat going through puberty. I rub my eyes, trying to dislodge the memory of swirling lights and unaccountable frustration. Yet another crater dream.

"Maybe the next meal."

"You've been in here for hours." Saida leans over my shoulder. No one would have guessed she spent the morning driving around looking at decaying animal remains. That's the thing I find most inspiring and simultaneously irritating about Saida: no amount of death and gore can stop her from cooing over an adorable baby. "Watching for reapers?"

"Trying to find footage of that crater." I lean back, rubbing my eyes. "I found one file that they meant to delete but missed. I keep hoping there's more."

"What did that footage show?"

I find it just as hard to describe the footage to her as I did when trying to explain it to Colin. "Blinking," I say finally.

"Like a buffering glitch, but massive, and colored like an acid trip."

"So, not helpful."

"Not really. Look at this, though." I pull up a spreadsheet. "StellBio's people went missing longer ago than StellBio said—between six and nine months ago."

"How do you know that? Their personnel records are lost."

I gesture at the screen. "Cafeteria inventory." She looks impressed and I have to hide a smile. "They had to log all their consumables," I continue, "and those numbers start plummeting about nine months ago."

"That is interesting, really, but don't you think you should take a break? Come on, come meet Ripley."

"There's more." I bring up a text file. "This came up in connection to one of the two cameras that used to watch the volcano. The cameras and almost all their recordings are missing, but the incident reports written based on what those cameras caught are still in the system."

She squints, reading it. "A captive thunderer went up the volcano and disappeared?"

"It doesn't say it died," I emphasize. "It just left the herd and vanished, eight months ago."

"'Presumed missing'," she reads in a whisper.

"And it wasn't the only one. I've found two other cases where a tagged animal went up the slope to the volcano and didn't come back. In all three cases, no remains were found, and all video footage from all cameras on that date was deleted."

Saida straightens, frowning. "And if it happened to the tagged animals, it's a safe bet it was happening to the wild ones, too."

"It's the volcano," I insist. "I don't know if it's erupting something or emitting something or what, but I think the volcano is having some kind of effect on the animals on this island, and I think it was affecting the StellBio employees, too."

She shakes her head. "A dormant volcano, though? Doesn't it seem like it ought to be something else?"

I should tell her about the dreams. I was able to tell Colin; why can't I confide in Saida?

I barrel on with my theory. If Saida is going to think I'm crazy, she may as well hear the full story first. "Notice how StellBio never claimed the missing animals died. No remains were ever recovered."

"So?"

"So, that's not just a crater full of weird light—it goes somewhere."

She gives me a pitying look. "Rosa, it's a 130-meter drop into a crater bigger than Kilauea. I think the more likely conclusion is that things fell in and died."

"Then why hide it like this? It wasn't just their research subjects, it might have been their people, too! Why delete the footage?"

"We don't know for certain that they were deleting files."

"I know," I say grimly. "Trust me, I've been sorting through their stuff for days."

"Exactly, Rosa, days of missing footage! I don't think one strange file is enough to prove anything."

"So why conceal it?"

Saida spreads her arms. "Because it was deleted on accident? Or by coincidence? I know it's weird—very weird —but I need you to focus on tracking the predator pack. Learning their movements must be our highest priority if we're to protect the thunderers, all right? Then we can focus on the volcano."

I rub my eyes again. My drone hasn't reported much. So far it's only located one hunting pair, and there's no sign of the main pack. "Right."

"Thank you."

"Have you been having weird dreams?" The question could jeopardize everything, but I need to know.

She blinks, taken aback by the change of subject. "I usually don't remember my dreams. But now that you mention it, I might've dreamed about a rainbow or something last night. Why?"

"No reason." Three for three. "Probably not getting enough sleep."

"Don't work too hard, then?" Her tone is gentler; I think she's genuinely worried about me.

"Okay."

"And you really do need to go see Ripley. She's—"

"The cutest thing." I slump forward, resuming my endless scroll through StellBio's labyrinth of files. "I will."

We never had pets growing up. My friends' cats seemed to hate me, while their dogs knocked me over in their attempts to befriend me. Once I moved out, my life felt too hectic and unstable to involve something as dependent as a pet.

Seeing Ripley, though, I almost get it. She is incredibly cute. Colin has built a makeshift pen by circling several upturned desks, and Ripley, who's about the size of a cocker spaniel, clambers around inside, chirping. I toss her tufts of the pink grass that Colin picked for her and she makes contented chuffing sounds while she eats. Her turquoise scales still resemble down more than scales, but she's already growing a thin coat of golden fungus along her spine. If she can be returned to a herd, the fungus will hopefully spread across her entire back.

Saida comes back in. I expect her to be delighted that I took her advice and visited Ripley, but she's frowning distractedly.

"Can I talk to you?" she says in an undertone.

I follow her out into the muggy afternoon. "What's wrong?"

"I trust you. You know that, right?" She looks into my eyes, as if she's willing me to see some deeper truth in her words.

"Saida, what's going on?"

"I found your missing aliens."

"Pardon?"

"Well, I didn't find them, but I found records of them. All the artificially-bred animals were tagged, right."

"Right."

"And loads of the data on those tagged animals was deleted, like your security footage."

"Uh huh."

She looks anxious. "We assumed it was to cover up some kind of loss or error—a mass die-off from disease, perhaps, or a genetic defect—but I managed to find the identification numbers for those specific creatures."

My heart starts to pound. She actually believed me. "And?"

"They're marked as missing—not deceased," she says. "And the tracking data is incredibly thorough: their exact locations are mapped out for their entire lifetimes, every step they ever took, and then their paths just...end."

"And they end at the crater."

"Yep."

I step closer. "Saida, you have to admit that we might have found something huge here. Something that might explain why

StellBio deleted everything they could and went dark."

Because they were dreaming, too; because everything and everyone here, sooner or later, wants to see what's in the light.

She chews on her lower lip for a moment, and when she looks back up at me again, her gaze is resolute. "All right," she says, "let's go see for ourselves."

The rover is intuitive and easy to handle despite its size. We keep the glass canopy open to feel the tropical breeze on our faces. Within twenty minutes, we've reached the juncture: left to return to base, right to proceed to the volcano.

I turn right.

The jungle closes in around us as we drive inland. Purple branches hang heavy overhead, their shade pink. The cool ocean breeze is replaced by oppressive mugginess.

We haven't spoken to each other since we left the facility. I'm not sure either of us knows what to say. What we suspect— what we might discover, and everything it might imply for Janus, for StellBio, for us right now—it's too much for words.

Without warning, we reach the tree line, and then we're heading up the steep black slopes of the volcano. The road looks disused, and deep fractures split through large sections—probably caused by seismic activity, but after everything we've discovered today, I wouldn't put it past StellBio to have attempted to destroy the road.

When the summit finally stops advancing towards us, I stop the rover. The observation outpost is a few meters east of us, a little metal cube perched on top of a lattice of struts. According to StellBio's power schematics, that's where a camera used to be. Aside from the file of crater footage I found, everything that camera ever saw is lost.

We get out and begin to walk towards the outpost. I feel an unsettling sensation of physically reaching the horizon, that the edge of the world is just a few steps away. My heart is hammering. I'm about to see something StellBio has put a lot of effort into me not seeing.

And the crater I've been dreaming about is about to come into view.

I look at Saida, who nods encouragingly. We scramble up the rest of the slope, palms scraping on the rough stone.

Two stories below us, a pool of shimmering light spreads out across the caldera. It's the root of a rainbow, liquefied gems, a quantum weaving of light and color that feels as warm and pleasant on my face as sunshine. Even though I've never seen it up close, it looks exactly the same as it does in my dreams. I half-expect to hear my brother's voice next, crying out to me from the depths.

The recovered footage didn't come close to conveying how beautiful—how alluring—the crater is. There are still many blanks to be filled in. What's in the crater? Why did StellBio try to hide it?

And why do I keep dreaming about it?

I kneel. I barely feel the sharp edges of the crater digging into my knee. The lights are so close.

"Rosa." I start; I'd almost forgotten Saida is next to me. She, too, is staring down into the crater, its glow sparkling in her eyes. "You brought your drones, right?"

"Yeah."

"Send one in."

I stand and take a few steps backward, as if a small amount of distance could protect me from the crater's thrall. I summon two of my drones from the rover and bring them up to hover by me at the crater's edge. I park the first on the pole where the original StellBio security camera was and program the other to dive into the crater. I say a little prayer that the drone won't immediately be disintegrated by volcanic gases and watch it plunge into the light.

"Well, what's it seeing?"

"I'm giving it time to collect data," I tell her. "We don't just want to see what's down there, but how far it goes. I went with power longevity over quick results."

Saida nods. She gazes into the light as if trying to pick out the drone. "Right. Smart."

I feel like I'm reliving my dream, vivid déjà-vu combined with an aching sensation of destiny. The lights look like mist at times, other times like swirling water. Again, I yearn to touch them, to know what they feel like. I stick my hands in my pockets, trying to counteract my longing with the tactile feel of cloth.

At some point it occurs to me that I'm hungry, that we should go back and get some dinner. I turn to say this to Saida and realize that the light around us is different. The sky is on the verge of sunset. Have we really been standing here for hours?

Saida looks at me, blinking, like she's trying to remember my name.

"Ready to head back?" I say, forcing cheery reassurance into my tone. I might be afraid of this crater—and rightfully so—but I'm not letting that fear take hold of me. In fact, in the warm glow of the crater, the fear is unsettlingly easy to push aside.

"Sure." Saida smiles, but I know her well enough by now: it's a forced smile, the kind of smile you put on when you want someone to believe nothing is wrong. A smile just like mine.

After dinner, I resume the same routine that I've been following since we arrived on Janus: clean up and file archived security footage until I fall asleep at my desk.

Or at least that's my plan, until I leave the cafeteria and find Huy standing outside, staring up at the volcano. Clouds thickened as night fell, and now the sky over the volcano is lit up with rainbow flashes of light.

"Huy?" I ask gently. Of the four of us, Huy has been the most reticent, even more so than me. We know that he taught microbiology at Berkeley for many years, and he sees the Janus mission as his last hurrah, his final professional achievement before retiring to wine country. Colin joked about getting more time with 'the missus', but that made Huy go still and somber, so no one brought it up again.

He faces me. Maybe it's just the dim lighting, but he looks like he has tears in his eyes.

"Do you ever think about what we're doing here?" he asks softly. "The lives we might change, if we can bring StellBio's research home? The fates we might reverse?"

I think about my brother sending me a message from light-years away to tell me that cancer claimed our father. I think about perpetually cheerful Colin suffering through the same maddening dreams as me. I think about whatever might have happened back on Earth to make Huy respond to mention of his wife as if he'd been physically struck.

"It's the opportunity of a lifetime," I say tentatively.

He waves me away. "You were headed somewhere. Don't let me keep you."

"Have a good night." I walk away slowly, casting a glance over my shoulder every few steps. He's already gone back to staring up at the volcano.

I have my hand on the door to the security office when my bracelet pings me. Instead of the friendly message alert, though, it's a blinking red light: an indicator of disaster.

I rush inside and bring up the drone interface. The drone I sent into the crater is gone. As part of its failsafes, it transmitted everything it had recorded as its power levels plummeted, then vanished.

Someone knocks on the door, then enters without waiting for my answer. It's Saida.

"Figured you'd be here," she says. Then she notices my screen and her face lights up. "Is that from the crater?"

I nod. Saida does a little dance in place. "Play it!"

I can't tell if the recording is distorted like everything else on the island, or if this is really what the volcano looks like inside: we see only churning white, intercut with static, and the occasional bright flash of blue or gold that shakes the camera. There's no sound; the mic must have been damaged.

The camera shakes more violently and the colors surrounding the drone begin to take form: tall stretches of steel blue, clumps of green, sparkles of peach and silver. It all swirls into a dizzying spiral before cutting out altogether, showing us only blackness.

"Wow." Saida looks astonished. "How long did it take that drone to get back?"

"Well…it didn't," I admit.

"Rosa," she says slowly, "what happened?"

"The drone broadcast this footage upon its demise."

"Demise?"

"We know that volcano puts off weird energies—maybe they drained the battery, or damaged its gyroscopes—"

"Well then, StellBio did one thing right." Saida shakes her head. "They didn't go anywhere near the volcano, and we won't, either."

"Saida, no! This is even more reason for us to see what's down there!"

"Do you see what it did to your drone? You want to send people down there?"

I jump to my feet. "I'll go."

"No."

"I've been dreaming about it," I confess. "So is Colin, and I think you are, too, you just don't remember."

She looks horrified. "What?"

"At least let me send another drone."

"You want to continue exploring a gas-filled volcanic crater that puts out electronics-disrupting radiation and apparently has been influencing our minds—"

"We know that animals have gone down there—"

"And probably fallen to their deaths!"

"I have one drone available," I continue doggedly. "I can make modifications, strengthen it—"

"No. All available drones should be watching the reapers."

I turn away, rubbing the back of my neck. I'd completely forgotten about the predator threat; the drone currently searching for them hasn't found any further trace of them. That alone should have concerned me, had I not been so fixated on the volcano.

"Rosa, I'm sorry," she says. "Really. Whatever's in there... I want to see it as much as you do, but we have to be responsible. If that crater really is affecting our minds somehow, all the more reason to keep away from it. We lost hours up at the summit without realizing, remember?"

"Yes," I admit.

"We were sent here by StellBio's investors to get answers," she continues, "and the families of the people who worked here deserve answers, too. Besides, we have our own families to go home to."

My story comes to the tip of my tongue, weaponized, something I can use to get what I want: a mother who will never be proud of me, a father who died hating me, siblings who don't know how to talk to each other, and me, running back and forth across the world—and now across the galaxy—trying to avoid the memories.

I swallow it all back down. She's right that the inviting pool from my dreams is a dangerous unknown. I just would've thought that the Saida who's faced down lions and jaguars would be willing to explore it with me.

"I'm going to run some filters on this footage," I mutter. I don't look at Saida. "See what I can see."

"I'm sorry," she repeats. I still don't look at her.

The footage is a nightmare to clean up, and the readings the drone took along the way are useless. Whatever is in the crater, it contains radiation or energies that refuse to be recorded, parsed, or observed. The grayish shapes at one point take on the regularity of a skyscraper's windows; a splash of blue and silver suggests a sparkling waterfall. At one point I could swear I see a smiling face, but I can't make the image resolve, and my eyes blur when I try to make sense of what I'm seeing.

I'm able to glean one fact from my hours of editing: at the speed the drone was traveling, and the angle at which it was descending, it went much farther than the supposed 130 meters to the bottom of the caldera. When the footage cut to black, it wasn't the drone being destroyed—the recording continued for another hour, until the drive was filled.

There is no bottom to the crater.

There is no crater.

When I finally curl up on an empty desk late that night to sleep, I dream, not of a glowing crater, but of an endless well of light through which I might float. I spread my arms. I'm about to step off the edge when I wake.

My drone interface is pinging me. The drone I left parked at the observation tower was programmed to alert me if there was movement up at the rim—and something is moving.

I bring up the display and my heart stops. It's Huy.

I open the channel to the biology lab. "Colin, Saida—Huy went up to the volcano!"

There wasn't any point to calling them; even at top speed, the other rover can't reach him in time. I change the frequency on my bracelet to speak through my drone.

"Huy, can you hear me?"

He's only a few feet from the edge. The rover is just behind him. I adjust the settings on my drone, zooming in as close as I can on Huy. The picture is terrible, choppy with blinding flashes of color. The only constant is Huy's black silhouette, frozen at the edge of the crater.

"I hear you, Rosa." His voice is faint.

"Huy, it's not safe up there, come back."

"I—dreaming about it." He's so close to the volcano, his words are obscured in static. Even through the noise, I hear his voice tremble with emotion. "I hear—wife —forgiven—"

"Huy?"

He jumps.

The blinding flashes are too much; I have to end the feed. When Colin and Saida burst in, they find me bent double in my chair, sobbing.

"He's gone," I manage.

I feel Saida rubbing my back. I can't stop shaking. Deeper than my shock, stronger than my grief, is something shameful: anger. I'm angry at Huy for giving in. I'm angry that he found his answers before I did.

I'm angry that he's free, and I'm still here.

I wake up in the cool dawn, standing at the door, my fingers on the cold handle.

Was I sleepwalking? I've never sleep-walked before. It should make me nervous, but all I feel is frustration that I still can't touch the light.

Then I remember what happened last night, and I have to run down the hall to the lavatory to vomit.

I skip breakfast. I go straight to my office, but this time I don't dive into the video files. I dig into the tracking records. I pull up pages of mind-numbing information about radio frequencies, transmission distances, and circuits.

Someone at StellBio must have noticed. If the volcano was affecting the radio transmitters—or vice versa—or if it was influencing the behavior of the predators, someone must have noticed. If they did, though, that information is gone, like everything else that would've helped us figure out what the hell is happening on this island.

I stand and kick my chair across the room.

Of course, that's the moment Saida comes in, with Colin in tow. Colin looks like he's been crying.

"Tell her what you told me," she says gently. If she heard my outburst, or notices the overturned chair in the corner, she ignores both.

He sniffles. "I was dreaming about the crater," he admits. "I dream about it a lot. I told you."

"You did," I say. Saida shoots me an unreadable look.

"Last night..." Tears well up in his eyes and he clenches his fists. "Last night I heard voices. That hasn't happened before."

"What did you hear?"

"It was a lullaby." He looks down at his feet. "It was a lullaby my mum used to sing. She and Dad both died in a car crash when I was six. I hear them out there, though." He jerks his head in the direction of the volcano.

"But they aren't really there, Colin," Saida says. She looks at me like she wants me to back her up. "It's a volcano emitting strange energies that we don't understand yet. There aren't people down there. Isn't that right, Rosa?"

Logically, I know I should agree with her. Of course our loved ones are not calling to us from the depths of a volcano.

But oh, does it feel nice to hear them.

Alarms blare. For a moment, I'm not sure what is going on. Is this the fire alarm?

Then I look at my screens. The reapers are here. They're attacking the fence.

"Rosa, look where they are!"

"Yeah, they're *here!*"

"No, *look!*"

She points at the screen and I realize that the reapers are clustered at the southeast corner of the facility.

"The broadcast tower," I realize. "Our signal."

"Shut it down! Shut everything down!"

I flip switches and enter emergency passcodes. One by one, screens go dark.

"The power grid, too!" Saida snaps.

"What about the fence?" It's a twenty-foot-tall high-tensile wire mesh, tough enough to stop a charging rhino, but it's also carrying ten thousand volts of reaper-stunning electricity.

"All of it!"

She's the predation expert. I run to the wall and haul down on a massive switch.

The room around us goes dark. I only notice the electronic hum that's been hanging omnipresent in the air since our arrival when it goes silent.

On a wordless agreement, we go out into the hallway. Saida is armed with a dart pistol; she must have been carrying it this whole time. She leads us outside into the warming morning.

"It's quiet," Colin whispers. "Did it work? Did they leave?"

Saida leads us across the facility. The jungle surrounding us is silent. I keep my gaze on the broadcast tower, its red light darkened.

The reapers are gone. The tower is untouched; the fence seems to have repelled the predators, even without the electricity. Once we get closer, though, I can see damage: three-inch-long punctures through the taut mesh. There's blood, too—they were throwing themselves at the fence hard enough to injure themselves. Their desperation to reach us —to do this to us—makes me shiver.

"Rosa, of all of us, you're the best with computers," Saida says, carefully touching the punctures. "Do you think you can get the ship to power up?"

"Now?"

"We need to leave." She begins leading the way back to the security office, holstering her dart gun decisively.

Colin looks stunned. "But...we can't!"

"There's got to be a way to override the ship's programming and leave ahead of schedule," Saida says. "There must be a failsafe. They can't have just stranded us here."

Colin is shaking his head, wide-eyed. "No, I mean, we *can't*! We have to see what's in the crater!"

Saida stops and seizes his shoulders. "Colin, I know you want what your dreams are showing you—believe me, I know—" Her voice catches and I wonder what she hears in the light. "But there are things on this island trying to kill us and we are thousands of light-years from home. Right now we have to focus on surviving. Maybe after that, later, we can worry about coming back to study the crater. Okay?"

No one will be coming back; I know that in my bones. Once officials on Earth realize just how dangerous this place is, no one will ever pass through that wormhole again.

Saida releases Colin and keeps marching. She turns on a flashlight and leads the way back into my office. "So, Rosa, do you think you can get the ship up and running?"

"I'll have to power up to look for a failsafe," I say, gesturing to the dark screens. "And the ship was programmed back on Earth—it's possible there's no way to alter it on this end."

"We won't survive another two weeks here. If the reapers don't get us, the crater will."

"I know, it's just..." I turn away, pressing my hands to my temples, trying to think.

I feel her hand at the small of my back. Her touch pulls me back from the edge of panic. "We can figure this out," she says encouragingly. "Let me help you. Talk me through it."

I take a deep breath. "First of all, I'm going to need power."

"So boot up whatever systems we need —"

"I don't know enough about the systems. I'm going to have to turn everything on, and..."

She flinches. Turning the power back on means restoring the radio signals—and luring the reapers back. "And?"

"And work fast, I guess."

She nods resolutely. "I'll stay at the door and keep watch."

"We can send out a decoy," I say. "I have two drones left. We can attach radio tags to them and send them up along the coast. Hopefully they'll be more interested in that than in us."

"Good idea. Wait—where's Colin?"

I turn instinctively to the monitors, but they're still off. I see only my panicked face, reflected in multiple. Saida runs outside and I run after her.

"Do you see him?"

"Where would he go?"

Then we hear it: metal hammering on metal. We chase the sound as it echoes off the StellBio buildings, tracing it to its source.

Colin has climbed into the enclosure where the ship rests on its launchpad. There's barbed wire along the top of the fence, but Colin doesn't seem to have cared—a strip of fabric and drops of blood cling to some of the spikes. He's wielding a handaxe, a standard-issue component of the emergency packs in the rovers, and drops of blood fly from his arms as he swings, again and again, into the ship's underbelly.

Saida screams Colin's name. He doesn't stop swinging.

"It's for our own good," he shouts. "We have to see!"

Something hisses. A huge seam tears opens in the underbelly of the ship, throwing Colin to the ground and spitting shards of metal across the launchpad. Saida and I throw ourselves to the ground. I've got my hands over my ears, anticipating an explosion that never comes.

Saida taps my shoulder and I sit up. Colin is gone.

"He targeted the fuel lines," Saida says heavily. "Hydrogen. It's all in the upper atmosphere by now."

"Can we refuel?"

"There should be backup fuel cells…"

Her words trail off. She's staring at something over my shoulder. I turn to look.

The red light is blinking atop the broadcast tower.

We both scramble to our feet. A moment later, the remaining rover roars out of the garage, streaking north towards the volcano.

"Backup generator," I groan. "He switched it on."

"He's luring the reapers back. Bastard." Saida draws her dart gun again. "Back to security. I'll get the generator."

The brightly glowing monitors welcome me back. I catch a brief glimpse of the rover as it hurtles past one of the cameras.

I raise my bracelet. "Colin, you're going to get us all killed!"

"Maybe you have families to go back to, but I don't. I'm not losing them again!" He's crying, but I can hear him clearly. He's still far enough from the volcano that the signal isn't being disrupted. He's driving fast and the rover's canopy is open; the wind whips his hair across his face.

"Whatever you think is down there, it isn't your parents!" My heart races like I'm lying to him. Am I not hearing my own brother down there, aching for comfort? Isn't my family out there, too? "Come back," I continue through gritted teeth. "Help us. We can refill the ship and go home where we belong."

"You and—both know where—belong, Rosa."

Something catches my eye on the monitors: reapers, heading for the road.

"Colin, turn back! You've got reapers coming for you!"

"I can beat them." He's rocking back and forth, pushing the engine harder. "I can—"

There's a splash of red and a blur of scales and a scream. The trees in the background judder wildly, then come to a sudden halt. I'm left watching the reapers tear into Colin, then into the rover's instruments, then there's only static.

On the other monitors, I see the reapers coming for the facility. Then the power dies. I'm left in dark with the afterimage of Colin's face burned into my sight.

I tap quickly on my bracelet interface. The display unfolds blinding white in the darkness. I bring up the two remaining drones, not as bait, but as my eyes. They take up position along the northern fence. So far, the jungle looks quiet.

I look for Saida in the garage, but there's no sign of her. Dread fills me—has she left, too?

Then I see her jogging across the facility. A few strands of black hair have escaped from her headscarf, and she's carrying a squirming armful of turquoise and gold: Ripley.

"Why are the drones still sitting here?" she shouts.

"Why do you have the baby?"

"The security office is the safest place. We can barricade ourselves there until the reapers leave."

"They killed Colin."

She bites her lip and looks away.

"Saida, we can't stay here. This isn't normal predator behavior. Even I know that."

"You're right." She closes her eyes. "I don't know what the StellBio signal did to them, or what the volcano did to the signal...you're right, though. By now they've associated this location with whatever torment they're experiencing, and that's overridden all normal instincts. By now they've probably killed every other animal out there with a radio tag, so now the only remaining source of the signal is here." She hugs Ripley closer and looks at me. "So, what do we do?"

"Colin's rover," I say. "He didn't get far. If we send the decoys like we planned, we can reach it on foot."

"And then what?"

I take a deep breath. "What do you think?"

She hesitates. "Power or no, they're going to tear this place to the ground and then they're going to keep hunting for us."

I nod. "We need to leave."

She looks past me at the ship, as if about to argue that we can't leave, not with the ship damaged—but then she remembers there's another way out, or at least a way that doesn't end with reaper claws.

She shakes her head, as if she can't quite believe what she's agreeing to. "Then let's go."

Around us, the jungle is a cacophony of rustling leaves and reaper chirps. Maybe they're chasing the decoy drones' signals, maybe all of their madness is focused on the facility, but nothing attacks us.

We find the rover askew in the road, the canopy still open, blood everywhere. Saida wordlessly hands me Ripley and goes to pull Colin out. I turn, facing us both away. The creature is surprisingly warm; I assumed it would be cold and reptilian. It looks up at me with wide dark eyes and squeaks.

"We can go," Saida calls softly.

I hand Ripley back to her and take the wheel. The engine roars to life and I hear answering bellows from the reapers.

We launch out of the trees, off the road, and straight up the slope of the volcano. The treads skid and judder on the rock. I look back towards the facility and see flames: the reapers must have ruptured a fuel tank or torn into some old wiring.

"I guess we really aren't going back," Saida murmurs.

"We couldn't anyway," I remind her. She nods.

The morning has turned cloudy; a storm is blowing in off the ocean. The crater's glow sparkles against the gray sky overhead.

"What do you hear?" I ask. "When you dream about it—who do you hear?"

The smile she gives me is almost shy, like even after all of this she's still embarrassed to admit to her dreams. "I hear a family talking, and silverware on plates. It sounds like friends or family, but it's always faint. I can never hear them clearly. What about you?"

"My brother. David."

"What does he say?"

Sorrow closes my throat and it takes me a moment to answer. "I can just tell that he needs me. I never felt like he needed me before."

I bring the rover as close to the summit as I can get. I hop out and help Saida, who's still cradling Ripley. Some of the golden fungus has come off on Saida, leaving her shirt glittering. She doesn't let go of my hand after I help her down from the rover.

The fire in the distance is growing. Other roars and shrieks join the reapers' calls as the creatures of Janus flee the destruction.

Far below us, the reapers are sprinting up the slope.

"Maybe we were wrong." Saida's gaze goes blank and hopeless. "Maybe it had nothing to do with the signals and they just wanted to eat us all along."

"There's still a way out." I tilt my head towards the crater. Just a few feet away, the air is alive with color. The baby stares up at the sky, chirping quietly, as if she's afraid she'll scare off the lights.

The reapers are coming faster. Even at this distance, I can see their eyes rolling wildly in their sockets. Their furious charge up the slope is tearing them up;

they leave shiny black footprints in their wake.

Saida is shaking her head. "We still have no idea what's really down there."

Other reapers have caught up to us. Off to my left, one hisses and launches— but its claws slip on the uneven shale and it trips. Saida and I scramble closer to the edge, even closer than we went last time.

"Are you sure it'll be okay?" she whispers. She's squeezing my hand, and I shift my grip so I can hold her other hand. The baby lies between us, cradled in our arms, as Saida searches my face for confirmation I can't give her.

"No," I admit, "but we know what will happen if we stay."

She bites her lip and nods. Gripping my hands, she inches us closer, step by step, to the edge. Her eyes are locked on it, their obsidian depths reflecting the swirl of light in front of us. I let her lead; I've been ready to step into these lights since I first dreamed of them. I can wait a few more moments.

Maybe the family Saida hears around the dinner table is her own. Maybe I'll get to meet them. The possibility makes my heart feel lighter than it has in years.

"Take your time," I whisper to her.

She takes a deep breath. "I'm glad I got to see you again, Rosa."

She tears her gaze from the light and looks at me. I forget about the snarling hunters and the weight of the alien in our arms and let her black eyes carry us over the edge.

Light closes over my head. I can breathe it. It's warm and smells like fresh rain on grass. I can't tell how fast I'm falling, but Saida is smiling, and Ripley stays calm in our arms. Were the other animals calm when they made this journey? A flash of blue whisks past, swift as a fish, and the baby chortles.

More colors coalesce out of the white: the same steel-blue as before, but also spots of rosy pink, neon, and grassy green. The rigid expanses of steel-blue resolve around me: flashes of skyscrapers. I glimpse poppies, and sand, and brick. I see a green stone tower and a flying car. I see tundra and blue desert, forests and markets, luminescent waters, cities under stars and cities among stars.

We are going somewhere.

StellBio, I'm certain now, went there, too. The light called to them, one by one, and they answered. Saida tries to say something to me, but the sound doesn't carry; she sees that I don't understand and shrugs, still smiling. The baby's huge dark eyes catch the reflections of worlds.

And the falling isn't soundless, either: there's music, all of it, every beautiful note that's ever been played and some that haven't yet. There's the roar of waves, the hum of a desert highway, and the silence of snow falling. There's laughter over the clink of silverware. There's a lullaby. There are no faces yet, but I'm convinced we'll see them soon. Already they feel familiar to me—welcoming.

I hug Saida and Ripley tighter and we fall into everywhere.

"See Laura Duerr's story "What Lies in Light" online at Metaphorosis.
If you liked it, leave a comment. Authors love that!
Remember to subscribe to our e-mail updates so you'll know when new stories are posted."

About the story

"What Lies In Light" originally began as an answer to a contest prompt, but I couldn't let the story vanish into my hard drive after it was rejected. Shifting the setting from an Earth-based volcano to an alien planet let me play with all my favorite sci-fi world-building toys: how did StellBio reach Janus? What communication challenges would they face? What sort of work were they doing on the island? What's the ecosystem like? Is the air breathable? (For word count purposes: yes.) And what kind of person takes on a job investigating a shady mad-science corporation on a dangerous planet light-years from home? I'd never written any character as convoluted and flawed as Rosa, and I wanted to investigate other characters' reactions to the mysterious light that tempts them. Are their responses driven by faith, desperation, madness, or some combination of the three? Plus, it was fun to write a world where the weirdest thing going on wasn't the symbiotic relationship between turquoise alien cows and a fungus.

A question for the author

Q: Do you ever feel bad for what you put your characters through?

A: It's funny that this question comes up in conjunction with this story because this is far and away the cruelest I've ever been to my characters. This story has a high body count (actually, this is only the second story in which I've killed a character), a narrator with a pretty high degree of self-loathing, and three other characters who confront past traumas. But I like to think everyone except Colin (sorry, Colin) got a happy ending, somehow. In everything I write, I want there to be an element of hope or redemption, so while my characters may go through challenges, they survive them and conquer them, and hopefully inspire readers to keep conquering the darkness their own lives.

About the author

Laura Duerr is a social media coordinator and writer of speculative fiction. A lifelong Pacific Northwest resident, she currently lives in Washougal, Washington, with her husband, their rescue dog, and too many cats.

rubybastille.wordpress.com

The Dybbuk

Lewis Gershom

The lawyer tells Louis the item in the package once belonged to his grandfather. His grandfather's will states that three days after his first grandson's engagement, the grandson is to receive the package. Yes, the lawyer does know the contents; but no, she is not at liberty to divulge said contents. This is the grandfather who died when Louis' mother was in college. This is the grandfather who never met Louis' father. This is the grandfather for whom Louis is named. This is the grandfather Louis has never met, about whom he has heard few stories. The lawyer clears her throat as

Louis stands motionless before a wall of legal tomes. Her ten o'clock appointment needs to come in. Now, she says.

The subways are packed on the ride home, unusual but not unimaginable for this time of day. Louis' back aches as the train creeps through Queens. He clutches the package tightly against his chest and peeks at the faces of the other riders and wonders just how many of their grandparents they have known. His thoughts meander back to childhood, the bewilderment he felt as his friends ran across their lawns and hugged their grandfathers, who towered above them like cypress trees. What was it they were feeling? The sun glints off the glass apartment towers across the river from Manhattan, so different from his grandmother's old brick Brooklyn apartment where she lived surrounded by her spouse's belongings until the day she died. He takes out his phone and sends a text message to Lecia to let her know he will be home soon.

The train pulls into the station with a lurch, shocking him back to full consciousness. He gets out and walks the three blocks back to his apartment. The elevator is on another floor when he arrives, so he takes the stairs instead. Lecia is asleep on the couch, unusual for this time of day. The box opens easily and leaves behind a pile of yellow powder on the table. Inside is a leather-bound book. His heart races with anticipation as he opens it. The inside cover reads *This Book Belongs To...* And Louis can't read the rest. At least, he's not sure. The letters are Hebrew—he has seen this specific array of letters before, but he can't remember where. A flashback to third grade. Hebrew school. The teacher is singing the alphabet as she writes each letter. He sings along, trying to keep up with her, the letters in his notebook mere scribbles compared to her effortless blackboard calligraphy. The letters come back as he sounds them out. He realizes he is speaking his own name. *Of course*, he says out loud to himself. The previous owner of this journal and the current owner both have (and had) the same name. The next page is filled with more unreadable text—most likely Yiddish. While his mom taught him some slang and a few phrases that are especially useful after hitting one's head or stubbing one's toe, the truth is, he knows Spanish better than this. He could sit here with a

Yiddish dictionary and alphabet chart and be just as lost. Still, he mutters a profanity under his breath for not paying better attention during Hebrew school. He mutters a profanity under his breath at his mom for not teaching him Yiddish. He mutters a profanity under his breath at his grandparents for not teaching her more Yiddish.

Lecia stirs. Normally when she wakes up she does so very slowly, remaining in a state of half-consciousness for minutes on end before she is ready to respond to stimuli. But today she bolts up panting, running her hands across her face, chest, and hair.

"Where am I?" she shouts at Louis.

Sometimes she has bad dreams where she wakes up disoriented and needs to be talked back to reality. "You're at home. I'm right here," Louis says.

She tilts her head towards him and says, "Who are you?"

"It's me," he says. "Louis." Lecia contorts her face and shakes her head. When she speaks her voice sounds right but her accent is all wrong. She sounds like a movie extra from the 1940's.

"No, that's my name," she says.

"Lecia, it's too early for this," he says.

"How do you spell it?" she asks.

"L-O-U-I-S."

"I'm L-E-W-I-S," she says.

He starts to wonder if Lecia has well and truly lost her mind. "What's the last thing you remember?" he asks.

"I was lying on a hospital bed. My wife and daughter were next to me," she says. "Will you please tell me where I am? Why does my voice sound like this?"

"What do you remember before that?"

"The lawyer picked up my will at the hospital."

"So you thought you were going to die," he says, no longer fully committed to the idea that the woman in his apartment still has her sanity.

"Kid, I don't know who you are or where I am, but I'm going to need some answers."

She hops out of the couch, unsteady on her feet. Her eyes scan the apartment and land squarely on the journal. She pounces on it.

"Where did you get this?" she says. It is less a question and more a statement pointed like a gun at Louis' head.

Louis tries to stammer out a reply, but no words can escape his throat.

"Tell me!" Her voice booms across the apartment.

"It belonged to my grandfather," Louis says.

Here Lecia grows still. Her breathing calms and she edges towards Louis on unsteady feet. "What do you know about him?" she asks.

"Nothing!" Louis shouts, incredulous. "No one ever talks about him—don't act like you don't know this, Lecia."

"What were you doing with the book?"

"Trying to read it, obviously, but it's not in English," Louis says, the frustration from a few minutes ago seeping into his voice.

"And how did you get it?"

"He left it in his will for me. For three days after I was to get engaged."

"Oh my god," she says. "That idiot rabbi was right."

Louis and the person in the apartment, previously thought to be Lecia—hell, she *was* Lecia until last night—sit across from each other at the table, draining a pot of coffee sip by sip. Lewis, the person claiming to be Louis' grandfather keeps staring. Louis can feel the other man studying the texture of his hair, the shape of his chin, the way he walks, the way he pours the coffee. Whereas before Lewis was possessed with a frenetic, electrifying energy, he now seems subdued by the coffee. They have cleared up the where—Queens, New York City—and they have cleared up when—2019. The next question takes Louis by surprise.

"Is your grandmother still alive?" Lewis asks.

"Bubbe died over ten years ago," Louis says.

Lewis snorts. "Bubbe?" He says. "I can't believe my daughter got you using that word. She couldn't stand it when we spoke Yiddish in the house."

Louis doesn't know what to do with that statement and doesn't respond.

"What was she like?" Lewis asks after the silence.

"Sick, sad, anxious. By the time I was born she was already too old to...to..." Louis struggles to find a way to explain it in a way that won't sound like an insult; he settles on, "... do a lot of things."

"Figures," Lewis says, sighing.

Once Lewis has learned to use the bathroom in a woman's body, something with which they are both quite uncomfortable, he hatches a plan.

"You know, I didn't die that long ago," Lewis starts to say. "The rabbi from the hospital may still be alive. He will know how to send me back."

"What rabbi? What hospital?"

"I was desperate for more time on Earth so I asked him if there was a way to extend my life, a way to defeat the cancer. He told me that people had been known to do mysterious things by writing the right words, so I wrote some stuff in my journal."

"Okay...."

"But he also advised me to make amends with some people."

"Did he say why?" Louis asks.

"Just that the plan wouldn't work, at least not the way I expected it to."

"My mom told me you and Bubbe weren't religious," Louis says.

"I wasn't," Lewis replies. "But I also didn't expect to wake up moments after dying...forty years later."

Louis nods, officially having given up on the idea that anything about this situation will make sense. Lewis continues.

"Look kid, I didn't believe any of his *farkakteh* advice. But when you're desperate, you're desperate."

"I...think I understand." Louis says hesitantly.

"Do you have a phone book?" Lewis asks.

"Sort of," Louis says, pulling out a cell phone.

They find the name of the rabbi and the hospital he worked at in 1979. They find that he took a job leading a congregation in Midwood, Brooklyn, in the late 80's after serving as a hospital chaplain for years. Louis calls the synagogue and while he waits for something to happen on the other end, his grandfather gapes at the technology in the apartment. An answer. The rabbi is still alive, still working, and he can see them if they get there soon. As they are leaving, Lewis ducks into the apartment and grabs the journal. Louis hails a cab and grandfather and grandson are on their way.

The rabbi's office is small and lived in. It smells like every church or synagogue basement in the world. Is this what mosques and ashrams smell like too? Probably, Louis thinks. Come to think of it, Louis voted in a local election in a mosque basement in his early 20's once and it did smell exactly like this. The carpet is a yellow-green color, skirting the line between drab and retro. In fact, none of the office looks like it has changed much since the 1970's. For Lewis, this must be an island of placid familiarity after waking up last night surrounded by flat-screen televisions, handheld computers, electric cars, and who knows what else. The walls are covered in pictures of the rabbi with all kinds of people—some looking very religious, some secular, and even a few celebrities. Among the celebrities is a picture of Bob Dylan, but curiously it's from the *Slow Train* period. The rabbi's desk is piled high with papers, and Louis, never a religious person, wonders what exactly a rabbi does that would require this much organizing. He regrets the thought. Judging by the look on the rabbi's face he probably knows exactly what Louis is thinking. Louis realizes it's his time to talk.

"Rabbi," he starts to say, but his voice comes out just louder than a whisper. The rabbi adjusts his rimless glasses to give Louis some time to collect himself. "Rabbi, I'd like to introduce you to my grandfather."

The rabbi looks the body of Louis' 30-year-old fiancée up and down.

"We have a few, uh, what do you call it? Tran, transe—, transgendered people in the temple, but this is new for me." Louis wonders if this is a rabbi joke or if he is serious. Lewis cuts in.

"Rabbi, I don't know if you remember me, but my name is Lewis Gershom. I was a patient at Beth Hagan Medical Center in 1979. You were working as a chaplain there the week I died."

The rabbi looks at Lewis, adjusts his glasses, and a smile starts to spread across his face.

"You fought me so hard. Your daughter made you speak to me."

"That's right."

"It's patients like you that made me want to take this job," he laughs.

"Rabbi," Louis starts to say again. "This morning I inherited my grandfather's journal. A few minutes after I opened it, my fiancée woke up from a nap and she pretty much transformed into him."

"What did the journal say?" the rabbi asks.

"I don't know," Louis says tentatively.

"Did you bring it with you?" the rabbi asks.

Louis passes the old book across the table.

"There's some interesting stories in here," the Rabbi says. "Too bad the kid can't read it." He puts the book down, tilts his head so he can see above his lenses, and gives Louis a profoundly judgmental look. "I could teach you how to read some of this, if you wanted."

"How much would it cost?" Louis asks.

Before the rabbi can answer, Lewis butts in. "Don't shame the kid."

"Excuse me?" the rabbi asks, incredulous.

"You know what I meant. The kid can speak however he wants. That's why we're all here, isn't it?"

"I...I...," the rabbi starts to say. Lewis cuts him off.

"The whole neighborhood had something to say when my daughter was a kid. I see not much has changed." He says these last few words while trying to swipe the journal from the rabbi's hands.

The rabbi pulls back and flips through the book.

"Be that as it may, any grandson should know some of this stuff. If he's not going to read it, you should at least tell him. March 6, 1975 for example...."

"I'll tell the kid when I'm ready," Lewis says crossing his arms.

The rabbi takes off his glasses and rubs his eyes. His face is red when he puts the glasses back on.

"Lewis, answer me honestly. Why did you leave your grandson the book if you didn't want him to know about your life?"

"I didn't think I'd actually be there to see it happen, you schmuck." Lewis relishes in saying the final word.

To Louis' surprise the rabbi laughs at this and continues with his questioning. Lewis seethes in frustration.

"Tell me something, Lewis, did you ever make peace with your associates...like I suggested?"

"Would I be here if I did?"

"Okay," the rabbi says, and flips through the book again. "Did you write anything while you were having, uh, conflicts?"

"Don't patronize me," Lewis says, sitting back in his chair.

The rabbi takes out a pen and starts circling parts of each page.

"Don't enjoy that too much," Lewis says.

The rabbi passes the book back across the table, leaving the comment in the air. "Look," he says, pointing to his circles. "In Judaism, God goes by many names. Some people believe that when you write down one of God's names, even by accident, special, supernatural things can happen."

The air in the room is still. Lewis rolls his eyes, but Louis follows where the Rabbi is going with this.

"Did he discover one of these?"

"Indeed," the Rabbi says, smiling.

"Jesus Christ," Lewis moans, slumping in his chair.

"And it turned your grandfather into a dybbuk. Just like I warned him in 1979." He leans towards Lewis as he says these last words. Lewis hangs his head in his hands.

"What's a dybbuk?" Louis asks.

"It's the soul of a deceased individual with unfinished business on Earth. Only when the dybbuk completes his or her task can the soul be released and die peacefully."

"This is worse than when I found out about the cancer," Lewis cries out. Louis and the rabbi turn to face him. "I just got used to the idea of being dead; now I have to go back to being alive?" He sulks in the chair like a scolded toddler.

"It's not so bad," the rabbi says. "Once you figure out what your task is, you can return to rest."

"Easy for you to say, you've never had to do this before," Lewis shouts at the man.

"Just think, whom did you wrong before you died?" the rabbi asks, trying to deflect the last comment.

Lewis groans and gets out of the chair, storming towards the door, Louis in tow. They hear the rabbi's voice call out one last time.

"Wait, both of you," the rabbi calls. Lewis waits in the doorway, looks down at his feet, and then back up at the rabbi. The traffic noise on Kings Highway threatens to drown out whatever is about to be said.

"Lewis...after you died...was there anything—"

"What do you mean was there anything?" He draws out these last three words.

"You   know…um…what   happened next?"

"Are you asking me if there was an afterlife?"

The rabbi nods.

"You're looking at it."

"Just come over for dinner tonight," Louis says to his mom over the phone. "There is someone I need you to meet." She tries to put up a fight, gets afraid that Louis is cheating on Lecia, or that, she knew it all along, he's actually gay. She apologizes for this one after Louis reassures her that this is not the case. Why wouldn't she apologize for accusing him of infidelity? She says goodbye and the phone call is over. Lewis, by now accepting the title of 'Grandpa,' has been asleep on the couch all day. On the way home from the synagogue he fainted in the taxi but when he awoke he insisted on not going to the hospital. "Chalk it up to coming back from the dead," he explained.

Louis hopes that when Grandpa wakes up, Lecia will be back, almost as if this haunting is one big nightmare. But when he awakes, Grandpa is still there, examining the devices in the apartment, grumbling about this and that.

"Are you ready for this?" Louis asks.

"This wasn't a good idea," Grandpa says. "Your mom doesn't want to see me."

"Why not?" Louis asks.

"She was angry with me when I died. I didn't help her pay for college. And then there was the reason I died."

"Colon cancer?"

"No. I died of liver cancer. The cancer reached my colon, but really it was my liver. I had a drinking problem."

"She never mentioned that."

Another silence passes. Grandpa is wearing Lecia's sad face and Louis really wants to reach out and put his arm around her the way he does when she looks like this, but this isn't Lecia and Louis doesn't know how Grandpa will react to a touch. The doorbell rings and Grandpa snaps out of his reverie. Louis answers the door and Mom walks in. She throws her things down on a chair and looks around.

"Okay then, who is it that you want me to meet?" Louis wants to speak, but Mom interrupts. "Is Lecia pregnant? Is that why she looks so glum? Lecia, what's wrong?"

"Mom, maybe you should sit down. Over here, next to uh—"

Mom sits down next to the person she believes is Lecia. Grandpa gives her a good, long look before he says something.

"Why is she looking at me like that?" Mom asks.

"Rhonda, it's me," Grandpa says.

"You never call me that," Mom says. "What's wrong?"

"It's me…Dad," he says.

Mom moves away from Lecia on the couch. Louis knows he should get back to getting dinner out, but he wants to remain in the room.

"Mom, it's the truth," Louis says. "We spoke to a rabbi about it."

"What the fuck are you two trying to do? My dad died forty years ago," she says.

"Do you know what a dybbuk is?" Grandpa asks.

Mom rolls her eyes and says, "It's like a Jewish ghost." As soon as she speaks the last word her eyes widen, and she clasps her hands to her mouth. "No!"

"Get back to dinner, kid. Let me catch up with your mom," Grandpa says.

Mom and Grandpa sit in the living room talking for a long time. Louis hears

Mom doing a lot of crying, both voices repeating the words *I'm sorry* over and over again. When the crying stops, Louis puts out dinner, chicken with vegetables, and they join. While they eat, Mom catches Grandpa up on the last forty years. She tells him about how she met Dad, when Louis was born, what she did for work, when Bubbe died, and finally Louis' engagement. Grandpa looks happy to be hearing all of this. He tells Mom he thinks his task was to apologize to her and she agrees that this is likely. Dessert is not served because no one likes sweets, but everyone eats some cheese. Mom says a long goodbye to Grandpa and goes home. Grandpa helps Louis clean up and gets back on the couch.

"Well, kid, it's time for me to go. It was nice meeting you."

"Is that really it?" Louis asks.

"That rabbi said I had to settle my unfinished business. What else could it have been?"

Louis shrugs and says, "How do you know when your, like, soul will be ready?"

"Well, Lecia was asleep when I woke up, so I guess I just have to go back to sleep."

"So, you don't know?" Louis asks.

"No," Grandpa says.

Louis makes a face and scratches the back of his neck. He is old enough to know that almost no death happens without words left unsaid. Now is the time to say all those things that one wants to say to someone who is dying, but his mind is almost blank.

"Do you think we'll meet again, you know, when it's my turn?"

"Not if your death is anything like mine. Dying and waking up this morning happened in the blink of an eye. I didn't notice any loved ones along the way," Grandpa says matter-of-factly. Grandpa shrugs, and Louis doesn't know what else to do but shrug with him. "You'll have your girlfriend back by tomorrow."

"Fiancée," Louis says.

"Whatever." They shake hands. "It was nice to meet you, looks like you're doing great."

Louis thanks him and says goodbye, but Grandpa's eyes are already closed, sleeping easy on the couch. Louis finishes the dishes and gets in bed, ready to have the events of the last twenty-four hours behind him.

Louis wakes up from a dreamless sleep. He is used to dreaming, enjoys it most nights, but yesterday was so surreal that his rest was a welcome respite from the fantastic. He stretches, gets out of bed, and is relieved to hear the sound of silence. The experiment with Mom must have worked. Grandpa's soul was released, and when Louis walks into the living room, he expects to find Lecia asleep on the couch. To his horror, the couch is empty, but there is a note. The note reads *'woke up feeling strange, went to walk it off. Love, Lecia.'* Louis had hoped that he would get to see her, to explain ... well, whatever it was that she would need explained, but for now he is contented by the letter. He makes himself some coffee, eats some breakfast, scrolls through social media on his phone. After an hour, Lecia still hasn't returned. He calls her phone. The seconds between the press of the call button and the ring-tone feel like an eternity. There is a buzzing noise across the room, and Louis puts it all together. The experiment failed. The phone is still in the apartment because Grandpa doesn't know what a cell phone is and didn't think to take it with him.

Louis begins to panic. His grandfather is missing. Except he's not his grandfather, he's the ghost of his grandfather's soul. Except he's not a regular ghost, he's a dybbuk, because he's Jewish, and if Louis tries to explain it to someone they are just going to say, *How is that different from a regular ghost?* He wonders whom one calls when a ghost inhabiting the body of a thirty-year-old woman has been set loose. The theme from *Ghostbusters* starts playing in his head, and he wonders why he is like this. He starts sprinting around the apartment, turning over every piece of paper, every book, any object that might indicate where Grandpa went.

Louis picks up the phone and calls the rabbi, but there is no response. He calls Mom and she doesn't pick up either. He puts on his shoes and runs up and down the block, then the adjacent block, then the block after that one, peeking into store windows and even cars trying to locate Grandpa. He sees some cops and considers asking them for help, but then thinks better. He doesn't know how an old Jewish man who last lived in 1970's Brooklyn would react to a couple of cops approaching him. It becomes clear that this is a lost cause. Despite spending the last day with him, Louis realizes that he still knows next-to-nothing about Grandpa's life. He doesn't even know what the man's job was when he was still alive. Why hadn't he thought to ask these things? An even worse thought flickers into his brain. *What if he took the journal?* Another thought... *Where did I leave the journal?* Louis runs back to his apartment, nearly taking down everyone in his path on the way. If there are any tourists out this morning they will surely report back about the crazed guy running down the street in a t-shirt, gym shorts, and leather loafers while the rest of the neighborhood is just waking up.

Louis scrambles to get through the door and bursts into his apartment. He jumps across the living room and feels a preternatural sense of relief when he finds the journal right where he left it on the coffee table. This time he notices that a bookmark has been placed between the pages. He opens to the entry. It was the one the Rabbi mentioned—March 6, 1975. The words are still incomprehensible. Louis still cannot read Yiddish. He tries to call Mom again to ask what happened on the date from the journal but she doesn't pick up. Louis slumps in his chair and tries to think of a plan. Fortunately, there is Google.

Louis sits hunched over his laptop and the journal. In one window on the screen is a chart showing which keys on a United States QWERTY keyboard correspond to which letters in the Hebrew alphabet. In the other window, a translation tool. He types each letter, one by one, until a disjointed, but readable narrative begins to emerge, mostly about Mom. According to the journal, he chose to break some news at the carousel at Flushing Meadow Park, one of her favorite destinations as a little girl. Predictably, she didn't take the news well. The journal entry ended there. With no other leads to follow, Louis stuffs the journal into his jacket, hails a cab, and makes his way to the park.

The scene at the carousel is worse than expected. Grandpa is having a full-throated argument with one of the operators. The ride has only just opened and it was okay that he went around a few times for free, but now that families are arriving he has to either pay or get off.

Grandpa tries to explain that he has no money. Security staff asks him to leave. To him, he is arguing with a kid who can't give an old man a break. To the carousel staff, a gentrifying white woman is trying to get a free ride. Grandpa sees Louis and waves him over.

"My fiancé will pay for the ride," Grandpa says. The fact that Grandpa is trying to get away with this makes Louis' blood boil.

"Let's go, Grandpa." Louis says.

"What did you just call me?" Grandpa says, doing his best impression of a hurt woman.

"Who are you people?" the operator asks.

"Do you have any money on you?" Grandpa asks.

"I don't want to," Louis says. "It's for kids." But he doesn't want to admit the obvious—this ride will make him motion-sick.

"Come on, your mom loved this thing when she was a kid."

"Grandpa—" Louis tries to protest but the ride operator cuts him off.

"You two are gonna have to either pay, or get the fuck outta here. Look at this line," the operator says. Louis and

Grandpa turn their heads to see the faces of a bunch of tiny children and their families staring at the bizarre domestic dispute happening before them.

"If you want to talk you will just have to get on here with me," Grandpa says.

Louis glares at Grandpa and hands over some money. Grandpa grabs Louis with surprising strength and drags him forward, telling him to sit on one of the horses that bobs up and down. Once the ride gets going, Grandpa waves at Louis to lean in.

"I'm not actually Lecia," he whispers. "I just didn't want to draw attention to us."

"Yeah, no shit, Grandpa. I figured that out myself," Louis says. "By the way, you don't have to whisper. No one can hear anything over this fucking music." Louis realizes Grandpa has nothing to say to this. "I read the entry."

"Already? You learn fast."

"So, what, you were just going to wander the city as some woman until I figured out how to track you down? You were just going to let me live like that? You were going to steal my future wife?"

"Not exactly," Grandpa says. "Once I realized that I had no idea how to get back, I figured I'd do some things that I missed out on before I died. This was at the top of the list."

"And then what?"

"And then I was going to go out, buy some clothes that I'm used to, get a job, and come back home to you." Grandpa says this as if everything sounds perfectly sane.

"You were going to go around dressed like an old man? Did you even bring money with you?"

Grandpa doesn't respond. Instead he starts to cackle, a laugh that comes out of nowhere and, turn after turn, wraps itself around the carousel. His smile, for the first time, is boundless. Meanwhile, things aren't looking so good for Louis. Each rotation of the carousel sends his stomach into a more rapid freefall. He doesn't know how much more of this he can take. Objects and images are starting to blur and seep into each other like watercolors. The music echoes in his skull. His heartbeat hammers against his Adam's apple. He wants to scream, but he knows what will happen if he opens his mouth. The laughter of the other kids on the ride penetrates his mind, and he breaks out into a sweat. He feels it coming. He jumps off the plastic horse and falls off the ride.

A security guard tries to secure him, but this is happening. Louis brushes past the security guard, runs over to the bushes and starts puking. The ground smells like sour coffee. The music has stopped. The spinning has stopped. He looks up to see who is putting the hand on his shoulder. It's Grandpa.

"Come on, kid," he says. Louis has no choice but to move along.

Grandpa leads Louis over to a hot dog cart, asks the vendor for a bun, a ginger ale, and two cups. Patting his pockets, he realizes that he has no money, so Louis pulls out a five-dollar-bill. They sit down on a bench and Louis grudgingly eats the hot dog bun, slowly, while Grandpa commences to pour the ginger ale from cup to cup and back.

"You know that's an old wife's tale," Louis says in between bites. "Ginger ale doesn't actually settle your stomach. People just give it to kids so they'll drink some liquids when they're sick."

"It used to work on your mom," he says. "I always gave this to her when she didn't feel well."

"I'm not my mom," Louis says, crumbs falling down his shirt.

"Okay then," Grandpa says. "If you don't want this, then I'll just drink it." He holds the cup to his lips and starts to drink. The vomit taste still lingers in Louis' mouth.

"Okay, okay," Louis says. "I'll have a little."

He passes the cup and Louis drinks until his mouth feels normal again. His stomach starts to feel normal too.

"While I was on the ride, I think I figured out what my quest is," Grandpa says.

"What's that?" Louis asks.

"I had this coworker that I never said goodbye to before they sent me to the hospital. We worked side by side for years and I didn't even wave at him on my last day of work. Do you think he's still alive?"

Louis can't take it anymore and says, "Fuck you."

"What did you just say?" Grandpa says.

"I said fuck you. I can see why my mom never talked about you. You're a real asshole."

"I just helped you with an upset stomach and that's all you can say?" Grandpa says, astonished at this man-child's *chutzpah.*

"We've been together for two days now and you haven't even called me by my name once!"

"It's confusing!" Grandpa shouts.

"You steal my fiancée from me, make me translate a bunch of pages from your journal, I manage to actually find you before you get yourself in trouble, and now just as I'm starting to feel better, all you can do is talk about some old-ass dead coworker." Grandpa looks away from Louis, sits motionless on the bench. He appears deep in thought, as if trying to foresee the rest of this conversation like moves in a chess game. "I'd rather throw up every day for the rest of my life if it means I can have Lecia back."

They sit side by side on the bench, Louis' chest heaving in a mix of anger and frustration. Finally, Grandpa breaks the silence.

"God, you sound exactly like my daughter."

"Real fucking mature, man," Louis says. He opens his mouth to speak, hesitates, and then goes for it. "March 6, 1975. What happened?"

"What do you mean what happened?" Grandpa asks. "You read the journal."

"No, I translated it. And I'm not a professional fucking translator of dying languages. So what happened?"

"I'm leaving," Grandpa says, getting up.

"Where are you going?" Louis asks.

"To get a job, an apartment, to start over. Clearly I'm not going back." After a few paces, Grandpa turns around to speak one last time. "I'm sorry, Louis. I'm sorry about everything."

As soon as Grandpa says this his knees start to shake and he falls to the ground. Louis rushes over and sees that even though his eyes are closed, he is still breathing and his heart still beating. Louis lightly slaps Grandpa's face and all of a sudden his eyes open. He helps Grandpa to his feet and leads him back to the bench.

"That's the second time in two days," Grandpa says.

"I can't have you injuring Lecia. I'm going to need her back...eventually," Louis says.

Grandpa sighs and says, "It was the day my mother died."

"What?" Louis asks.

"The journal entry. It was the day she died—the day I broke the news to your mom."

"What happened?"

"One morning I was at home with my mother and I decided to go out for a walk. To make a long story short, when I got back, she had fallen. Her skull split open."

"I—" Louis tries to say.

"So I called your grandmother, the police, the ambulance, the whole nine yards. Your grandmother came home and dealt with the rest of all...that. I drove to your mom's school, picked her up, and drove her here to break the news."

"How did she react?"

"She was furious. Furious that I didn't take her to see the body, furious that I came alone, furious that I left her grandmother alone in the house. That it was my fault."

Louis looks at his feet. The story more or less matches the translation he cobbled together. There are no real surprises.

"But the worst part, for her, was the way I broke the news. She felt like I was treating her too childishly. Like she couldn't handle it."

"I just can't believe I'm learning all of this now," Louis says. "From a ghost."

"I know you feel alone in the world, but it's not that unusual," Grandpa says. "Look...you never knew your grandfather, your mom never knew her grandfather, I never knew mine, and your grandmother never knew hers."

"What are you trying to say?" Louis asks.

"Listen—my parents each came to this country as children, alone. I don't know how they met because they never spoke of their lives before me and my siblings were born. While they were here, giving birth to me, my grandparents were most likely getting killed in Poland. Maybe by Russians, maybe by Germans, nobody knows."

"Really?"

"My parents had nobody to help raise us kids and before anyone knew it, they were too old to take care of themselves. My father died long before your mom was born and then my mother moved in with me and your grandmother. I had to support the entire family."

"And then?" Louis asks.

"And then I died. Only a few years after my own mother. I never got to have the life I wanted." Louis wants to say something, but there is nothing he can say to follow this up. He feels bad for calling Lewis an asshole, for refusing to get on the carousel. Grandpa starts to speak again. "I knew that I wasn't going to live long enough to see my daughter grow up, really grow up. But all those years where I was going from one room, to check on your mom, then back into the other to check on my mine, all I could think about was how I would never get to meet you."

Louis is shaken by the gravity of this information. It's heavy information, yes, but one piece of information is still missing. He asks, "how does the journal fit into all of this?"

"I had hoped that my additions to the journal would give me another few years— maybe just enough time to see you as an infant."

"So why leave it to me?"

"I knew my wife and daughter wouldn't talk much about me. I expected someday you would get curious about me, just as I did about my grandfather. This way you would have the chance to know me at some point, at least, in my own words."

"But...then why couldn't you be nicer to me? Why didn't you try and get to know me?"

Now it's grandpa's turn to cry, but he's a man from a different time and men from a different time don't cry. He wipes his eyes, inhales deeply and looks away.

"Life is complicated, Louis. You never know who you're going to disappoint." Louis thinks he understands, but a part of him knows he'll never understand completely.

"You said you hoped for the chance to see my birth," Louis says.

"Yes."

"Can I tell you about my life now?"

When Louis finishes telling him about his childhood, his friends, college, Lecia, and his job, Grandpa's eyes start to dim. He grips the bench and leans back, struggling to keep his head upright. Louis shakes him and tries to say something, but Grandpa's head falls back. Louis lets out a long exhale, hoping that this is finally it. Grandpa's eyes flash open and Louis flinches in fear.

"God damn it," Grandpa yells. "I really thought that would work."

"The fainting spells, that has to be it, right? You have to be getting closer."

"I don't know, kid. I think you're just gonna have to get used to me."

Louis racks his brain for a solution. He digs deep into his memory, trying to unearth any hidden recollections of his brief religious education that might reveal a solution to this particular problem, but most of his memories of that time revolve around Pokemon cards being passed below desks like contraband. Louis shrugs and pulls out the journal.

"I'm borrowing this." He says.

"For what?"

"If I'm the task, there should be something about me in here. I'll write something. Maybe then you'll be able to go back."

Louis writes for a few minutes, putting down every detail that he can remember. All the while, Grandpa leans over his shoulder. Satisfied, Louis puts the journal back in his pocket. Grandpa has been awfully quiet. He shakes Grandpa's body, and waits for Lecia's eyes to open.

"See Lewis Gershom's story "The Dybbuk"
online at Metaphorosis.
If you liked it, leave a comment. Authors love
that!

Remember to subscribe to our e-mail updates so you'll know when new stories are posted."

About the story

Early in 2019 I was spending time with some family members and I overheard a story about a friend-of-a-friend who, through somebody's will, inherited a bunch of old belongings. This friend-of-a-friend assumed they were to receive something of sentimental value, or any value, but it actually turned out to be, literally, a massive pile of junk in an attic. It became this person's unfortunate responsibility to clean out the attic.

The idea of a family inheritance turning out to be a major inconvenience intrigued me. I wondered what it would be like if I were to receive an inconvenient inheritance. What would that item be? In what way would that item be inconvenient? Drawing on family lore and this simple idea, I set out to write what could best be described as a Jewish ghost story. The protagonist of this story receives an item that reveals to him the source of his family's idiosyncrasies and his position in the greater Jewish diaspora.

A question for the author

Q: Are you a Luddite? Or do you have the latest and greatest technology?

A: As someone who teaches computer science to children and manages technology for adults, I am often mistaken for a great lover of technology. The truth is that I try to get to know the latest and greatest technology as well as I can so that I only have to use it sparingly. My computers all run GNU/Linux and I use open source whenever possible. I don't bother with 'smart home' technology, but I love Raspberry Pis.

About the author

Lewis Gershom is a writer of speculative fiction. He writes about the issues he sees in his hometown of New York City. When not writing, he teaches middle school English and computer science.

Notes from the Laocoön Program

Phoenix Alexander

The orbital module fails to detach and we ignite in the full-mouth kiss of the planet's atmosphere, spinning with a velocity that pushes us to the black brink of unconsciousness. G-force grinds us into seats molded for our forms. There is the view through the porthole in my periphery – of jittering flame and cartwheeling stars and the glowing edges of unfamiliar continents – and the interior of the capsule in front of me. My vision breaks, the views looping into kaleidoscopic fragments.

I do not panic. I trust in my training. Anything can be controlled: my breath as my body is buffeted by forces huge and inhuman, and the focus of my vision as it lightens with the threat of unconsciousness.

The combined mass of the disintegrating orbital module and our descent module is too much for our parachute to bear. I am calm as it shreds in the force of re-entry, incendiary rags streaking the black beyond the porthole. Sparks fall inside the module, too; orange nodes of slag burrow into my legs. There is a hot meat smell, but I feel no pain.

The planet's surface comes rushing up, patches of harsh white vegetation rippling across its surface and I see something move beneath the earth, as if the chalky ground were a skin over something far more alive, and vast. For a moment there is the nightmarish impression of skin pulled taut over a face the span of an entire world. I am drunk with adrenaline – and I *brace*.

The successful firing of the landing rockets is a small mercy. The capsule finally hits the planet's surface and my spine, elongated after months of weightlessness and beaten by the tumbling violence of our descent, breaks. There is pain – and then pride as I identify which vertebrae have shattered (they are somewhere in my cervical spine, perhaps C3 and C4, where my neck meets my shoulders). Beyond the porthole: fire.

The memory is of a hot and starry night on a date on which something is celebrated, I forget what, because in this memory you are the most important. And in this memory I clutch in my hand a little burning thing. Nothing loud or dangerous, just a sparkler, flaring fire as I draw words in the air: words I will never say to you but that I pray you can make out.

Kiss me, Brian Lowe, I write, laughingly. You always hated your name for being too dull. To me it is miraculous. *Kiss me.* The words hang in afterglow between us and then disappear. You are bolder than I, living a happiness that I envy. Entirely comfortable in your skin. Yours was a happy childhood, free of the scandal of your mother deciding to love women when you were in high school. *You* were not bullied by children as cruel and judgmental as their parents – though not as cruel and judgmental as my father, who tried to 'beat the queer' out of my mother until, one day, she simply left.

You would never call yourself that, would never define yourself by your most intimate desires. You are just *you*. You, laughing, the beautiful contours of your face lit by the sparkler as you dodge backwards.

"Stop it, you'll set my coat on fire," you smile, grabbing my wrist. The moment is a gentle kind of control and your breath is warm.

So I stop writing the words, and I don't say them. I have the feeling of a moment passing. Of some kind of threshold being crossed, an alarm in my mind blaring to announce that *time is up*, and I don't know why I felt that and I am full with regret.

I say this to you instead: I am moving to California for Test Pilot School and I am asking Alice to marry me. Because I can't tell you that I am my mother's son, as shameful and perverse as she. I won't label myself as she did, though, giving ammunition to those who would spit out the word like shrapnel, like my father, weaponizing a private act until it signified something as far from intimacy as it can be... I just love you, and I don't know what that means or how I would live it, but I love you anyway. I don't say any of that.

Anything can be controlled.

Your face tells me everything I need to know in that instant and I see the lie reflected back to me. You withdraw your hand and my skin feels the loss immediately.

The horrible thing is that, still, you never looked so beautiful. I do not know if the sparks in your eyes are your own or from the sparkler I hold like a white flag, still burning, between us.

I must have lost consciousness briefly. My eyes peel open to smoke roiling across the surface of my vizor and Mikhail yelling in my earpiece. The capsule has landed us on our backs and, amazingly, the thing is in one piece. I look up at the million blinking buttons of the control panels: all red, all furious. There is a line on the computer command transcript that indicates a control override on the orbital module, but I issued no such thing. I *would* not. There must be a mistake. I close my eyes, seeing nothing but pulsing black. The black begins to glow orange and I open them again. Flames have now spread to a conflagration in the view beyond the porthole to my right. The planet's surface beyond is an unlikely plain of tiny, white-headed flowers with fat stamens, and squat pills for leaves. We have burned a great black patch through them and streaked the earth with the violence of our landing. To my left: my companion, Mikhail, fumbling at the harnesses with an uncharacteristic clumsiness that is the only sign of his discomfort.

I attempt to shift in my seat. Nothing happens. My limbs do not work.

"Mikhail," I say. My voice is a poor, croaking thing. "My back is broken." I don't know if he hears me so I say it again. "My back is broken."

I see Mikhail's eyes narrowing through his visor and I know it is bad. He unclips and peels the belts from my torso, crusts of melted polymer falling like confetti upon my shoulders. He says something and my ears ring, the sounds taking sluggish moments to coalesce into something intelligible.

"Don't move. I need to look outside."

I see his lips move and make out the word *outside* and hear it in comically slowed syllables (*ah-ooh-tsai-duh*). I visualize him stepping onto a planet of flame, a little David in the face of a fiery Goliath the size of a world. Perhaps it is the endorphins, the adrenaline making me feel invincible even as my insides clatter nausea.

I speak to him to control it.

"Sounds good. Check where the fire is."

Mikhail climbs over me towards the entry hatch above my head. I peer into the polycarbonate bowl of his visor as he passes. I want to raise my hand, folding the fingers until just the thumb sticks up: the classic gesture – just to do *something*. I cannot. So I give him a smile instead. Bravery in the face of the infinite unknown. He returns the gesture, pulls at the hatch above my head, and crawls out into a new world.

"You have a slightly erratic psychometric profile," they tell me.

I ask them to explain, precisely, how my psychometric profile is 'slightly erratic.'

The Chief of Operations answers. He is a powerfully built and diplomatic man who has completed three spacewalks in his career – yet who is still, as far as I'm concerned, prone to lapses of appalling stupidity.

"Well… if you're asking. You never admit your errors. You blame everything and everyone else: your colleagues, the engineers, the computers, equipment. You have bouts of rage – usually directed to female staffers. You –"

"Enough."

The Deputy CO silences him and the two exchange glances while I stand very still, crushing my lips together, because to move them at all would probably cost me my career.

A lesser man would have snapped.

A lesser man – yes, you – would have smashed both of their smug faces in, and the smug faces of everyone on the damn committee, sitting at the table like morons.

"The fact of the matter is," the CO is saying, looking back to me with something of a smile on his face, "that despite these… judgments, you are the perfect individual for the mission."

I leave confused: insulted, prideful. Staccato footsteps follow me down the corridor and when I turn, the Deputy CO is on my arm, her face so close I can see my reflection in the water of her eyes.

"Huxley," she whispers. "You don't have to accept this mission. I'm just saying. You can walk away."

I remove my arm from hers.

"Why would I?"

"You wouldn't be the first. There would be no shame."

"I'm not like other people. I'm not afraid."

She looks at me as if to say *you are exactly like other people* and I snap my head away before I do something I regret. Her voice wheedles behind me:

"Just... know that you don't have to say yes to this."

What does she know? Hasn't my whole life been leading up to this? All of my hard work, my training, my discipline?

Of course I say yes.

I am still, packed in my chair with the interior of the capsule crushed around me. My knees should be throbbing with pain, crushed almost up to my chin. My bones should hurt and my skin should ache and burn but instead there is nothing.

I am not worried.

I am only a little lonely at the sight of Mikhail's empty chair right next to me. Our in-suit comms work, at least, and he speaks to me breathlessly through my earpiece in lilting English.

"How are you doing in the gravity?" I croak. I wet my lips with sips of water, the straw curling over my shoulder into my suit.

"Ok."

There is the harsh sound of Mikhail's breathing as he stops speaking. I watch from the porthole. I see him straining with each step, padding through the grass around the capsule, and I lose sight of him for several minutes. Then he comes hobbling back into view.

"The capsule is ok. Not going to burn. But... "

His voice trails off. Instead there is his breath, and another breath, and another, each heavier than the last.

The breaths quicken.

"Good," I reply. I take another sip of water, swallowing hard. "But what?"

I watch him stop and force himself to stand at full height, looking around him in all directions. The sky is a rusty haze above him. Pale clouds of ammonia ice string the air like entrails. His heart rate accelerates in my earpiece along with his breathing, our spacesuits sharing biometric readings.

"What? What do you see?" I ask him.

"We – there must be some mistake," he says.

"We don't make mistakes."

"This is not the planet we were trained for."

"You're wrong." I say immediately. "Its mass and radius are what we expected. Same for the surface gravity. The atmosphere is –"

"*Listen*, Huxley. Someone has made a mistake."

Ice-cold agony needles between my shoulder blades and burrows into the base of my skull. The pain is so great my vision greys.

"What do you mean, there must be some mistake?" I manage to say.

"This is not the planet."

"Have you contacted Mission Control?"

He nods. "Nothing. The line is broken or something."

The image of the command code overriding the orbital module rolls green in front of my vision, and with it the awful possibility that *they know about this*. The pain softens, as if something warm has nested in the base of my skull. I do not tell Mikhail. His panic would be the end of us.

I watch him kneel (the movement quick, the planet eager to bring him to its surface) and pull an instrument out of his suit, sinking the needle into the soil. "Calcium, silicon, and iron make up the highest percentage of minerals..."

His head suddenly cranes to the right. He has seen something behind him – something I cannot, no matter how fiercely I squint.

"Mikhail? Mikhail, what is it?"

He freezes, stuck in a crouch.

"Huxley."

"Yes."

"I think I see something."

"What do you see?"

The radio crackles and his words break, infuriatingly. "... someone... hell..."

More harsh breaths, more heartbeats. I do not want to know him so intimately. His pale suited body stretches, then stiffens, caught between rising and –

what? Crawling? Away or towards the capsule? He is a good man but an idiot, a coward, indecisive at the worst moments.

I lose my temper.

"Be a man and tell me what you fucking *see*," I roar even though it shreds my throat. The tip of the straw hits my lips. *Fuck it.* I snap at it with my teeth: the only movement I am capable of. I admit: here I lose a little control.

"What do you see? What do you fucking *see*? No, no, don't come in, don't..."

Then he is gone from my view, and there is the sound of the hatch being hauled open behind me and he clambers over my body and falls into his seat, babbling in Russian and hammering at the displays.

"Чужеродная форма жизни обнаружена ... Слушаю ... Чужеродная форма жизни обнаружена, отвечайте пожалуйста ..." There is no answer, from anything, from any quarter. Mission Control is silent.

"Careful!" I shout to him as he jostles me. I know it because I can see my body moving but I feel *nothing at all*, not the impacts, nor the weight of his body.

I have to slow my breathing because I know I will lose consciousness; the panic will send me down. One of us has to be strong.

He falls into his seat, hammering at the controls and at the comms panel on the gauntlet of his suit until, eventually, he calms. I look back out of the porthole. The flowers billow in a deepsea waltz, white dust tumbling in the wake of Misha's footsteps. I can see nothing beyond.

You can't blame me for being angry.

You would be probably dead by now.

I ring my wife and tell her the news. The insults from the CO, the Deputy urging me not to take the mission – the disrespect shown – got to me, I must confess. The moment I dreamed about since childhood sours and seems banal, strangely predetermined, as I tell it to my wife. Perhaps it is because it is her I am telling it to and not you.

"Just let it go," she says. "Focus on the positives. My God, Hux! You're going to *space*."

She is cheerful. Suspiciously so.

"Are you sure you're ok with that? You aren't going to miss me too much?"

There is a pause on the end of the line.

"Sure," she says finally.

"You don't sound convincing."

"What do you want me to say, Hux?"

"I – never mind. Bye."

I hang up.

I make another call.

Your voice is sleepy, as if you were sunbathing, sunblinded. I try not to visualize your body.

"Hey, Brian."

"Oh! Huxley…"

I tell you about the mission and the comments from the Deputy.

"Don't worry about it," you say. I can hear that you are beaming and I smile, too. "You're the coolest, calmest man I know."

"I thought so too."

"How is Alice?"

"Oh, she's fine."

"Good. Is her writing coming along well?"

I realize I don't know how to answer him. Instead another question tumbles out of my mouth before I can stop it.

"Are you seeing anyone?"

There is a pause that breaks my heart, because I know the kind of answer that is coming. "Well... yes, actually."

Of course, of course you are. That's what people do. My fingers lock on the receiver.

"Oh? What's her name?"

You laugh again, slightly unsure this time. The sound is cruel to me. I am not smiling anymore.

"Jaeyoung. His name is Jaeyoung."

Part of me is stunned, truly, for the first time in my life. Another part is not surprised at all and accepts this like a death. This: the loss that was traced in the air that night with the fireworks, when I was too afraid to say how I wanted my life to be. With you.

I want to say a million, an infinite number of things, each word a red jewel of something – what? Anger. There is only anger. Anger, anger, anger, pulsing in syllabic form and ready to fall like a meteor.

I hang up.

Mikhail is asleep in his seat next to me.

I am glad for his presence. I do not know the time; I cannot see my watch. It has been perhaps two hours or ten since we crashed.

I go over the launch, scouring my mind to find what could have happened. We checked and tripled checked the mechanisms every step of the way; I could not have made a mistake. My fingers found the keys by rote, the checklist running like a biometric display before my eyes. Everything was working perfectly. We ran simulation after simulation and it all worked, everything worked, nothing predicted this.

Someone did this to us deliberately. We were sabotaged.

The Deputy CO. It must have been her. That bitch! That's why she tried to warn me... but why? Why?

I try and move the fingers of my left hand. Nothing.

I try and move the fingers of my right hand.

Come on

Fucking come on –

My index finger twitches. Sweat falls into my eye. I try harder. This time it moves more. The fingers almost – almost – curl a little, as if around a beer can.

I stop trying. My breath comes in gasps and the sound frightens me. It sounds like something else: less than human. Sweat pours into my eyes and between my lips. I can't touch any of the buttons or dials inches from my face to call Mission Control, my wife, anyone. I can't do anything.

A scream rises. I clamp my teeth shut.

I am not screaming in front of Mikhail.

I am not screaming in front of *anyone*.

So I wait for the moment to pass.

Something moves before my eyes.

In the quartz glass disc of the porthole, in the flowerlands beyond, under a dim sky where the stars shine brilliantly: the plants have changed. The petals of the flowers seem to have withdrawn, or closed. I squint, but the distance is just too great to see clearly, and my eyes sting from the sweat. I look out into a forest of gently undulating pearl-white fronds that move, awfully, rising up from the ground like hairs on aroused skin.

"Mikhail," I say.

He snores and whimpers into his helmet.

The fronds move, blown by a wind I cannot fathom, and turn to gesture in the direction of – us. I feel observed.

"Don't you dare," I whisper. I want to make fists with my hands. "The fuck... the fuck is this?"

Yes, I am losing my cool. You always thought I wasn't aggressive, but you're wrong, Brian, you're so wrong. You helped me control it. I never got angry in front of you. But you are not here. You aren't here, supine, broken-backed, on a foreign planet and watched by things like snakes, half-alive, looking at you with pearly tips with no eyes but *you know they are watching anyway* –

You would be screaming by now. I know you would.

Mikhail speaks next to me and I cry out.

"Huxley," sleep-thick he speaks, "why are you crying?"

Then he looks out of the porthole beyond me and shouts in horror.

"Go out there. Go out there and kill them," I yell.

Instead he fumbles for the controls. Speaking to Mission Control, reporting these things in frantic Russian that cannot be true ("Nine meters – no, ten, eleven, ah, I think they are alive, yes... please send help, please help us...")

The comm is silent. There is no one there.

While I shout and curse at him Mikhail turns away, crushing himself even further into his seat, and simply stops looking.

"What kind of a miserable fucking coward…" Rage saves me. I curse him instead of screaming my fear. At some point exhaustion shreds my voice so I, too, close my eyes.

White limbs wave endlessly in the black in front of me and I think I hear a voice from the comm, the CO's voice – "… satisfactory… independent variable…" – and I think, *What on earth can be satisfying about a forest of fronds glowing and growing and watching, without even orbs for eyes?*

They tap instruments against the wet membranes of our eyeballs, testing the pressure. We run on treadmills at the bottom of an Olympic-sized swimming pool meant to simulate exercising in zero-g; the pressure makes my limbs iron and my breath come hard through my oxygen mask. They attach other masks to our faces and pump increasing levels of CO_2

into our respiratory systems: 2 mil, 3 mil, 4mil. We are sat next to one another in doctor's chairs, me and Mikhail, and he whimpers with terror as the mask is pulled over his head, whereas I take it with a grim smile. I would take anything this way. To serve the greater good.

Could you say that? You, who gave into your baser desires and who even now are probably growing fat and complacent in an unremarkable job in an unremarkable house with an unremarkable man – a *man*! Jaeyoung. The word circles in my head as the CO_2 levels pump up to 5mil. Mikhail starts coughing beside me, eyes streaming. I hit the arms of the chair with my fists.

"Who the fuck is Jaeyoung anyway?"

The orderly looks at me.

"Pardon?"

I rip off my mask.

"Mind your fucking business," I reply.

They hold mock funerals for us, as they do for all astronauts. Afterwards the psychologists ask me questions that I have never heard an astronaut asked before.

"Do you believe in the dignity of non-human life?"

"No."

"What aspect of death frightens you more: physical injury or the concept of the oblivion of consciousness?"

"Neither."

"Which is the stronger force: love or fear?"

I do not answer – I cannot answer that – because to me there is no real difference. But I do not tell them that.

I wake up to Mikhail crying.

At first I think it is something calling outside – but I know that is impossible, because all my senses are filtered through my suit and come with an underwater muteness, or with a tinny crackle of the comm, or they don't come at all. My eyes open and there it is: the round porthole a meter in diameter, my entire world coming through this circle. The flowers are still there, fat and stupid. The terrain rolls like a crumpled bedspread. As my eyes focus, I see odd patches where the flowers have been crushed – as if something has dragged its belly across the ground in a meandering path, or a line of animals has trampled them. The paths disappear into the distance in a crazed path.

My lips work for the straw. The flesh of them feels cracked.

"What is it, Mikhail?"

At first I don't understand what he says. Then I do.

"I have been tasted... something tasted me..."

"What are you talking about?"

"I woke and something was pushing my back like, like a knife in different places and my suit is..."

His voice trails off. I can tell by the direction of his voice that he was – is? – looking at his seat. I see his dim form hunched in my periphery. I try to move my head a fraction and am stunned by the agony.

"Чёрт!" he curses. Again and again.

"What? What? What is it? I can't fucking move..."

"The *seat*!" he shrieks. "Full of holes! There is something beneath the capsule, there must be something beneath the capsule in the ground..."

The image of that titanic face returns: gaping its mouth as we fell, streaming fire, pushing up against the surface of the planet to take us, sending tendrils up to taste...

Without warning, he squeezes over me again. I can't feel the mass of his body, but he knocks my knees and legs and I shout to him *"Stop, fucking STOP,"* because he could be doing more damage to me but he is over and out of the hatch again, shoving it open. And he is outside.

"Mikhail, stop…"

I hear the impact of the hatch rolling to behind my head, sealing me in. I do not scream. You'd be proud of me, Brian – I don't scream. Out loud, at least. I want to move. I want to move my fingers and toes and pull myself out and run to you, thousands of miles away, on the planet I call home. I want to hold you in my arms and feel the warmth of your body and tell you I forgive you for Jaeyoung, and ask for *your* forgiveness in return for betraying you with my sham of a marriage, of a life.

But I cannot move. And so I watch Mikhail stagger over the terrain through that goddamned porthole, bent double under the weight of his own body, his breathing and heartrate alarms in my ears. And something else: a warning tone, electronic this time. A red, glowing visualization of his skeletal structure pops up in the inside of my vizor. And a numerical reading, negative 2, that I do not at first believe. Our suits perform scans of our bodies every 24 hours, sweeping us with minute levels of radiation – and his bone density reading is almost equivalent to someone suffering from osteoporosis.

Impossible.

The suit must have been damaged. I look from the display to the pitiful sight of him clambering over distant dunes outside, headed for God-knows-where.

Nothing makes any sense.

"Mikhail. Your bones..." I share the visual feed with him, although no doubt he has already been alerted by his own suit.

"Tasting!" he shrieks. *"Tasting!"*

I remember the cold finger of pain and the wending warmth at the bottom of my skull and wonder, too, if I have been tasted: if tendrils have pushed up from this planet, somehow burrowed through the combined layers of metal and insulating material that make up the outside of the capsule and pushed into my body, tearing the fibers of my suit and tasting, taking mass...

There is movement again outside. Not Mikhail, and visible through the ground-hugging carpet of white dust he leaves in his wake. A head peers up over a mound of terrain in front of him.

A human head.

And another. And another.

They move as one over the hill and come for him.

Dust kicks up in a cascade as he turns to run – but the gravity is crushing, and the creatures, backs bent in parabolas, haul themselves with horrible speed. I can see the muscles of their arms from where I lie here: they are like elderly men and women curled by age, palely human, hideous. Their eyes are big, bulging from their sockets, their heads downturned and necks craning down to the ground. Their backs are the highest parts of their bodies. The spines curve and push upward like the hulls of capsized ships. Their pupils are quick and agile, moving in their broad and horrible homogenous faces. They shamble in pursuit of Mikhail, faster than they have any reason to be. I hear their shrieks and cackles over the comm. They seem to be enjoying this.

They seem – happy.

There is screaming and screaming. I cannot see beyond the pillar of white dust that rises in the distance: the only signifier of Mikhail. Rocks clatter (or is it teeth?) and a final scream arcs up, high and womanish, before the comm goes quiet. I stop screaming as he does. I listen. His heartbeat is audible – accelerating to almost 200 beats per minute – and accelerating further. Then all readings go dark.

They must have torn him from his suit.

My heartbeat is my own.

I bring up the display of my own biometrics in the corner of my visor and find that my bone density is at negative 3 (how can that be possible? How?)

Now that I think about it: why on earth would our suits measure bone density? Why didn't I ask?

...I have been tasted. I have been taken from.

I am alone, on my back, with the planet drinking from my spine, betrayed by those I thought I could trust. They have killed Mikhail. They will not kill me.

When the dust settles I see his spacesuit, torn in two pieces, lying among the flowers.

Perhaps there is no use but I speak into my helmet, hoping someone will answer, hoping for a human voice in my earpiece. "We are being attacked. We are dying. I do not understand what is happening..." I think of you and I start to cry and I ask for help. I beg. It is easy: as easy as I was terrified it would be. For the anger to quench and the awful weakness inside to speak its truth, raw and shameful. "Please help us. Please help me. Please. Please. Please."

Someone clears their throat – I hold my breath for an answer – and there is an intake of breath (a woman, the Deputy CO? Will she be kind to me again?) but there is nothing, no answer.

"I know you're listening. I know you're *fucking* listening..." I can't breathe. My chest rises and falls too fast and what I think is my screaming is the breath trying to come and not coming. I fall blackly into unconsciousness.

It is the final meal with my family and friends before we leave for Star City. You are not there. I regret that now. Isn't that funny? Regret always comes too late. I don't think we are capable of regretting anything as long as there is a chance of turning things back, of changing them at any moment. Or so we delude ourselves.

And then the chance is gone, and there it is: regret. The most useless of things.

So we eat, and you aren't there.

There is Mikhail and his wife Isabella, and an Italian astronaut whose name I forget, and my wife and her sister, and her sister's husband and their children. And Mikhail's friends, two men, and their wives, and their five children between them. We toast in our various languages, the adults laughing over vodka while the children crawl and clamor around our legs.

"I tell you," Isabella beams at me. "You're lucky you don't have kids. It's hard, leaving them behind."

I smile and think of you and drink.

"Isn't it funny," my wife says, pink-faced tipsy, "that they aren't letting our husbands dock on the Space Station? Just a shuttle up there, strapped in for the journey, and then shot back out to this very, secret planet on this very, secret mission."

Isabella hiccups. "I heard that the planet is changing location. Can you believe? The thing is *moving*? Planets don't do that."

"Well..." My tongue feels thick and my head hurts. I wonder how much I should bother to explain to these women. "We discovered it about 20 million miles from Venus. It has an erratic orbit – which planets undoubtedly *do* have, and..."

A child grabs my trouser ankle and I yelp, almost spilling my wine. Isabella is no longer listening – perhaps she never was – and leans into my wife, who catches my eye across the table. I see pure wickedness in her as she speaks. "I mean, honestly, Hux would probably smash something vital the moment something pisses him off. Months of precious scientific research ruined because my husband can't keep his temper."

Isabella claps her hands.

"Yes, and my poor Misha would wet his suit when something goes wrong – can you imagine? Putting poor Hux through a faceful of his zero-g piss..."

The women laugh. Mikhail, to my disgust, grins like a fool next to his wife.

"It's ok, I'll just piss on him in the capsule," he gestures to me.

Poor Hux.

"What exactly *is* your mission?" one of Mikhail's friends asks. Mikhail shrugs, laughing like everyone else.

"Data collection, assessment of habitable environment, you know."

The friend laughs, the sound foolish. The man's lips and teeth are reddened from wine. "I don't know, actually. But it's ok. I get it."

Poor. Hux.

I stand up. This is intolerable.

"Here we go," my wife says, leaning back in her seat.

"Yeah, here we go. I'll tell you what our mission is. It's advancing the progress of fucking mankind. How is the writing coming along, darling? Sold anything yet?"

The laughter stops abruptly.

"You know," Isabella interjects. She is not smiling anymore. Her glare is sober. "I always wondered why you married him, Alice. What do you get out of it?"

"What does she get?" I can't let her answer. "This house? An income? Freedom to write those shitty romance stories that no-one wants to publish, let alone read?"

I regret the words as soon as they come out but it's too late, far too late. A child cackles from underneath the table.

Alice is unfazed and raises a glass to me. How I wish it were you there, raising a toast to me. About to say something kind. Not this. Not whatever is coming.

"Nicely put, *darling*. To the progress of mankind."

Somehow that is worse than an insult. She did not lose control; she won.

She drinks, her eyes not leaving mine over the rim of the glass. Toddlers rough away, trampling food into the carpet around the ankles of the adults. You are not here.

I hear nothing further from Mikhail. I can see no sign of him outside, nor the ghastly creatures that took him. My comm picks up nothing. I roar and howl into it, screaming for Mission Control, screaming for *someone* to come and get us.

"Mikhail is dead, Mikhail is dead," I tell them over and over and over, and then, I think it is the nighttime, but who the fuck knows on this piece of shit planet with no day or night sky but that endless, star-pricked, white-blue? I hear someone clearing their throat again over the comm and I go to scream louder – but then I am tasted again. Indisputably.

The whole capsule moves. Something is pushing up from the earth and into my bones. Through insulator fabric, through metal, through glass that has withstood the fire of a planet's atmosphere. The view in the porthole shifts to that sky again, and the flowers... the flowers rise with me.

I think I make noises of terror. I don't know. I watch as the white eyeless tendrils push up through the seat next to me and the console panels crack and break and the worst thing is that they are alive, they are sentient, and I know they are hungry for a body I thought was mine and mine only.

I look out of the porthole and the planet has grown a million tendrils, a million limbs, and the flowers aren't flowers at all, and among and within the glowing forest I see the humanlike creatures that attacked Mikhail and Mikhail himself – is that him? Naked and bent, loping over the ground with an expression of such happiness as I have never seen on a human face!

The capsule jolts in the air and my head moves.

I can move! I can move! I can...

I look down my body for the first time since our landing. The tendrils have pushed through my arms and legs and out of the tops of my knees. Two heads, eyeless, featureless, white and glistening, nod from each patella, inches from my eyes. *How awful it is to have one's body violated*: I think I should feel that. Yet I feel nothing at all.

What did she see in me? Why did she marry me?

The sex wasn't there from the outset, but she didn't seem to mind.

I asked her once, in the early days, when I felt bad for not taking her like a lover as often as I felt I should.

"It's okay. I don't mind. I'm not much interested in sex anyway. I just like your company."

Why did I forget that?

She liked my company.

But I always felt hated. I always felt that hatred came from her, but perhaps it was always from me.

I hope she didn't hate me.

I know she didn't. If I am honest. I have not been honest for a long time. Perhaps for my whole life.

My father never believed in our marriage. I think he always knew. The cocked eyebrows when I embraced Alice in his presence, the wry smile.

"How is your friend Brian?" "When are you gonna make me a grandad, Hux?"

I avoided his questions every time. Laughing them away the way men tell a joke to hide something raw.

I wonder what my mother would have said.

Why was I afraid? Why couldn't I be kind to the friend that Alice was, if nothing else? Why not kindness?

I have made a ruin of my life and for nothing at all, for a feeling that I am unloved and must stay that way forever. Perhaps the measure of life is how kind we are.

And I have not been kind.

I must have lost consciousness, because I wake and the capsule is on the ground and my body is whole. The flowers nod outside. The stars shine. The ground is white dust rolling between them and there is Mikhail's suit, torn in two pieces still.

There is a voice.

"Huxley. Huxley Davis. Hux."

It is a voice I have heard before.

"Brian?"

The name is clarity. I feel light, as if I will blow away in the easiest cosmic wind.

"Not Brian." A name I recognize. A woman. The Deputy Chief of Operations. This time her voice is not unkind, not mocking. Her words come quick and breathless and sibilant but not unkind. The opposite of that. "I shouldn't be calling you but I... this is cruelty. I can't be long. Listen to me. You were supposed to fail. You all were. That is why you were chosen. There is a creature living under the planet's surface... the planet *is* a creature. A creature like nothing we've ever seen before, and one that feeds on human matter. You weren't supposed to come back. You weren't supposed to survive – because you couldn't. You have too many weaknesses. That was the point. Do you see? That was *always* the point. We wanted to see the effects it would have on the weakest of us. What it wanted. What it *still* wants."

A tear rolls down my cheek and all I can think of is your face. I see the sparkler. I see fire.

"Calcium," I whisper. Bone-white light films my eyes. The creatures, brilliant men and women wrecked with the symptoms of osteoporosis and rollicking as happy and content as idiots across the surface of this monstrous world. "That's all it wants. Calcium. I'm an astronaut. I..."

The weakest of us.

I know she is right. I know.

The mission is not so heinous, really.

Dulce et decorum est, pro scientia mori. "Why didn't you just tell me? I would have died for this mission. My body... everything. I don't care. I don't have much to live for. I would have come here willingly."

There is silence on the comm. Something like weeping.

"...There is a letter for you. From Brian Lowe. Your wife sent it to us here. Would you like me to read it to you?"

I can move my hands. Slowly, and the fingers are curled and the elbows don't move. The creature in the planet has taken calcium from me. It's alright. It is a good price to pay. I think of Mikhail's face and the happiness there. I think of what is on Earth. And I think of the voice here, in my ear, about to read your words to me.

"Yes." I don't know if I say it out loud or just wish it, or just dream it, but there you are: in a woman's voice, over dark space, thousands of miles away, but there you are, there you are, there you are.

Dear Hux,

I know you probably don't want to hear from me but I had to write.

I never blamed you. I want you to know that. I *never* blamed you.

But I needed you to be a little braver for me. I couldn't wait for you anymore. God, it hurts to write that, but it is true. Do you hate *me* for that? I think of that and I am ashamed. I can't sleep at night sometimes. Maybe I should've waited just a little bit longer, until you felt safer. Maybe I should have pushed you harder when you told me you were marrying Alice. Maybe I shouldn't have been so afraid. But now you have your life, and are doing amazing things, and I am here on Earth trying to make the best of things too.

There is so much I want to say to you. But I'll stick to the most important because I never was good with words.

Huxley Davis: I want you to know that you are my one great love.

Yours forever,

Brian

The afterbreaths of tears on the comm. Then the Deputy says: "... he drew a sparkler at the bottom of the letter. It's in blue pen – the stick part – and lines scratch out of it in red pen so you can imagine the sparks. I wanted you to know that. ... Hux? Huxley, are you there? Huxley?"

I can move again.

The thing has stitched my nerve endings together with the flowers-that-are-not-flowers, with the fibers that have taken my calcium like alveoli taking oxygen: just a process that happens, without malice, to keep an organism alive. It is alright. Everything is alright. Turning in my seat, sleepily, like an ancient thing coming to life, I push out of my harness. With newborn hands I remove my helmet. The effort makes me sweat, because my fingers are curled and the muscles of my forearms are thin and taut. I press my face to the glass of the porthole. That damn porthole. I do not curse it now. I was a child looking out of it. I am not that anymore.

White-red light makes dazzling lines across my vision and I imagine you out there, you like you were that night all those years ago: young, bearded, beautiful, holding that sparkler out to me. This is it: this is the second chance.

Will you come with me? I imagine your voice saying to me.

Yes, my love. This time there is no hesitation, no fear. None in the slightest. None at all. *Yes.*

Well come on then.

I remove my suit and undergarments and crawl out of the capsule to emerge, naked and blinking, in starlight. My back is bent and my limbs extend rigid under me but I have never felt stronger. The air is as sweet and as new as I imagined air on a new world would be.

You are not outside, but the others are, and Misha crawls forward and touches my arm. He looks delighted, delighted, happier than a man has any right to be.

"Let's go, let's run," he says. Nodding. His chin tucks into his chest.

I raise a knuckle to a horizon distant and flower-filled. A million heads nod, making promises. The planet settles beneath us. Everything answers: *yes*.

I am doing this for you, because I know something the Deputy doesn't. I know what this planet wants, because I want it too.

It wants to not be alone. To take a living person into its most intimate core. To take many people, a million lovers and make them happy, but make them *stay*. It doesn't matter if we are the weakest humankind has to offer. Even the weak deserve a chance to be remade whole.

I'm not afraid now! I'm brave because of you. I see that now. Your love has done that.

Watch me!

Breaking into a run with the group who coax me on, because the gravity is stronger here, but do you think a planet's core can keep me from moving?

Watch me run!

Faster now, howling all my regrets to the windless air (my wife, my mother, my father, I am sorry) and the children I never had and the friends I pushed away and my family who don't matter anymore because *you* are here in my heart, just over that rise of earth, beyond the starlit horizon. My second chance, my angel, my family, my savior.

Watch me, loping life over the planet of a million flowers, breathless blesses from my lips dedicating each and every one of them – to you.

"See Phoenix Alexander's story "Notes from the Laocoön Program" online at Metaphorosis.
If you liked it, leave a comment. Authors love that!
Remember to subscribe to our e-mail updates so you'll know when new stories are posted."

About the story

"Notes" was inspired by a summer reading astronaut's memoirs in Southern California. I was struck by the 'Stepford Husband' superhumanity of the literary personae they presented - and wondered what would happened if you started to poke at the cracks. Then I imagined a spacefaring program that might look for something... different.

A question for the author

Q: What's your favorite story?

A: I crave 'quest' storylines that change their protagonist's worldviews over the course of the narrative. I need characters to somehow find hope, in whatever form that comes, in increasingly abject circumstances -even ones they would never have imagined themselves capable of surviving at the opening of a story.

About the author

Phoenix Alexander is the Science Fiction Collections Librarian at the University of Liverpool and curates the largest collection of SF in Europe. He is a queer, Greek Cypriot scholar and author of speculative fiction that is as much concerned with inner worlds as the spaces between stars.

phoenixalexanderauthor.com, @dracopoullos

Copyright

Metaphorosis Publishing

Metaphorosis offers beautifully written science fiction and fantasy. Our imprints include:

Metaphorosis Magazine
plant based press
Metaphorosis Books
Driftwyrd
Vestige

Help keep Metaphorosis running at
Patreon.com/metaphorosis

See more about some of our books on the following pages.

Metaphorosis Magazine

Metaphorosis is an online speculative fiction magazine dedicated to quality writing. We publish an original story every week, along with author bios, interviews, and notes on story origins. Come and see us online at magazine.Metaphorosis.com

Keep Metaphorosis running! Support us at
Patreon.com/metaphorosis

You can also find us at:
Twitter: @MetaphorosisMag,
@MetaphorosisRev, @Metaphorosis
Facebook:
www.facebook.com/metaphorosis

We publish monthly print and e-book issues, as well as yearly Best of and Complete anthologies.

Metaphorosis:
Best of 2018

The best science fiction and fantasy stories from *Metaphorosis* magazine's third year.

Metaphorosis
2018

All the stories from *Metaphorosis* magazine's third year. Fifty-two great SFF stories.

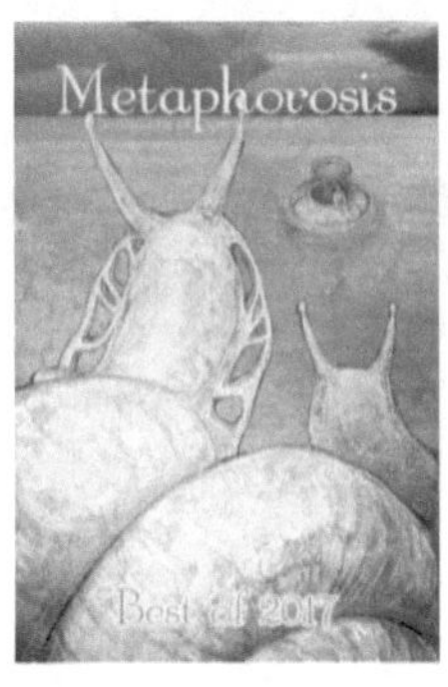

Metaphorosis:
Best of 2017

The best science fiction and fantasy stories from *Metaphorosis* magazine's *second* year.

Metaphorosis
2017

All the stories from *Metaphorosis* magazine's second year. Fifty-three great SFF stories.

Metaphorosis:
Best of 2016

The best science fiction and fantasy stories from *Metaphorosis* magazine's first year.

Metaphorosis 2016

Almost all the stories from *Metaphorosis* magazine's first year.

Plant Based Press

Vegan-friendly science fiction and fantasy, including an annual anthology of the year's best SFF stories.

Best Vegan SFF of 2018

The best vegan science fiction and fantasy stories of 2018!

Best Vegan SFF of 2017

The best vegan science fiction and fantasy stories of 2017!

Best Vegan SFF of 2016

The best vegan science fiction and fantasy stories of 2016!

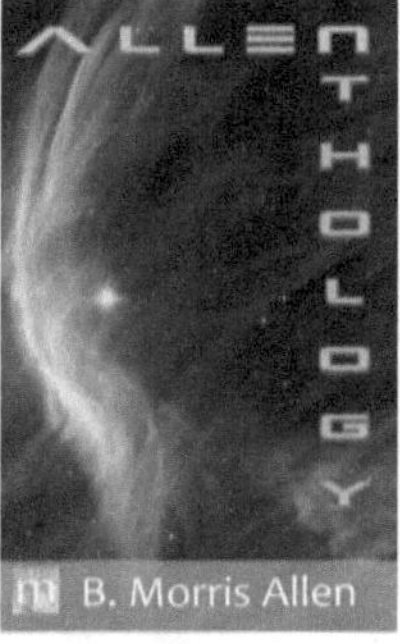

Susurrus

A darkly romantic story of magic, love, and suffering.

Allenthology: Volume I

A quarter century of SFF, including the full contents of three separate collections.

Metaphorosis Books

Science fiction and fantasy books for writers – full of great stories, but with an additional focus on the craft of speculative fiction writing.

Score

an SFF symphony

What if stories were written like music? *Score* is an anthology of varied stories arranged to follow an emotional score from the heights of joy to the depths of despair – but always with a little hope shining through.

Reading 5X5

Five stories, five times

Twenty-five SFF authors, five base stories, five versions of each – see how different writers take on the same material, with stories in contemporary and high fantasy, soft and hard SF, and a mysterious 'other' category.

Reading 5X5

Writers' Edition

All the stories from the regular, readers' edition, plus two extra stories, the story seed, and authors' notes on writing. Over 100 pages of additional material specifically aimed at writers.